The Outlaw and Other Stories

MOCHTAR LUBIS

The Outlaw and Other Stories

Translated from the Indonesian by Jeanette Lingard

SINGAPORE
OXFORD UNIVERSITY PRESS
OXFORD NEW YORK

Oxford University Press

Oxford New York Toronto
Delhi Bombay Calcutta Madras Karachi
Petaling Jaya Singapore Hong Kong Tokyo
Nairobi Dar es Salaam Cape Town
Melbourne Auckland
and associated companies in
Berlin Ibadan

Oxford is a trade mark of Oxford University Press

© Oxford University Press Pte. Ltd. 1987
Translated from the Indonesian Bromocorah
First published 1987
Third impression 1991

ISBN 0 19 588859 6

Printed in Malaysia by Peter Chong Printers Sdn. Bhd.
Published by Oxford University Press Pte. Ltd.,
Unit 221, Ubi Avenue 4, Singapore 1440

Translator's Note

MOCHTAR LUBIS, who was born in Padang, West Sumatra, in 1922, is a distinguished Indonesian journalist and author of international renown.

This collection of short stories was written in 1982 when he was invited to spend one month working at the Rockefeller Foundation's centre for study at Bellagio in Italy.

All of the stories in this book are based on real people and real situations encountered by the author over many years. Adaptations have been made in the development of the stories, but the basis is reality. For example, Mochtar Lubis met the man upon whom the character of 'The Outlaw' is based when he himself was a political prisoner during the Soekarno regime.

Mochtar Lubis has always been a fearless and outspoken critic of social injustice and the abuse of power both in society and between individuals. In common with most of his writing, this collection of short stories realistically depicts the conditions, experiences and situations against which he continues to protest.

Contents

Contents

CHAPTER ONE

The Outlaw

HE got up very early and went quietly out of the bedroom without waking his sleeping wife. He had been trained to move without making a sound. It was a skill he had to have in his work. He opened the door slowly and silently picked up his pants, black jacket and big belt that were piled on the seat near the door, put on his leather sandals, and closed the door again. When he went out the back he looked at the couch in the middle room and saw his eight-year-old son, still asleep, covered up in his sarong.

He opened the back door and washed his face with water from the big jar in front of the kitchen. He dressed quickly and then walked briskly out of the village.

It was still very early, before daybreak. The village still slept. Not one dog barked when he passed by. They all knew him. He quickly crossed the stream at the edge of the road, climbed up on to the narrow path through the rice fields at the river's edge and walked nimbly along it. The terraced rice fields rose higher and higher following the slopes of the hills.

The morning mist was still low on the hill tops and the breeze blew gently. He breathed in deeply, holding his breath for a while, then breathing out till his lungs felt empty. As he did this he kept striding along, synchronizing his steps with his breathing. He felt his blood flowing hotly, his heart beating strongly, his muscles starting to feel loose and warm, and the stiffness of his body after a night's sleep began to disappear. When he reached a field level with the top of the hill he stopped in the middle of it and looked around.

Dawn had broken. It was starting to get quite light. After he was sure there was no one else around, he stood and took up the *silat* stance, facing towards the rising sun. Slowly he moved his hands, his feet, his body, in the movements of *silat* calmly but smoothly. Gradually he increased the speed of his movements until at one moment in the dim dawn only the swift movements of a black shape could be seen. Anyone who suddenly arrived and saw the black silhouette turning, leaping up high and lowering itself to the ground would certainly be very startled and would not know that the black, fast moving shape was a human being.

When he felt his sweat starting to flow, he slowed his movements and then stopped, facing the sun which was beginning to appear behind the distant teak covered hills. He said a prayer asking God for protection, safety and strength. Then he stood and relaxed.

In his heart he felt pleased at the way his breathing was still normal after exercise like that. He was not puffing at all. Now his whole body, all of his muscles, were awake and ready. So were his senses; his eyes, ears, the whole surface of his skin, all were awake and alert.

Conviction of his own strength and skill in *silat* filled him. Then suddenly he turned, and moving quickly, climbed to the top of the hill. He climbed another hill and entered the teak forest and almost an hour later reached the middle of it. He began to tread carefully, taking care not to step on any dead, dry twigs or leaves lying on the ground. This was the place where they had promised to meet. He looked around carefully and saw nothing out of the ordinary.

In the small clearing in the forest it was a little lighter than among the teak trees. He sheltered behind a tree, crouched down and groped for a dry stick and threw it. The sound of it hitting a tree seemed loud in the silence of the forest. That sound was immediately followed by another one from the top of the tree. A peacock, startled from its sleep, flew off abruptly, moving far away to another tree.

At the same moment, from the corner of his left eye, he saw a shadow move and disappear behind a tree about three metres to his left. He smiled. He was pleased that his adversary felt the need for caution in confronting him. Slowly he dropped to the ground, blending himself in with the dark shadows thrown by the trees, and edged towards the tree where the figure he had just seen was hiding.

He was still one and a half metres away when suddenly a quick, black, moving shape emerged from behind the tree heading fast and hard towards him, accompanied by a shout, not very loud, but sharp and frightening. For a man inexperienced in *silat* combat that sound would be enough to freeze him for a few moments before he could move again, and in *silat* combat, freezing for a few moments could mean defeat or even death.

But he was an experienced *silat* expert. He was thirty-five years old and had studied *silat* since he was ten. His first teacher had been his own father, a feared outlaw. And then he had travelled around the whole of Java seeking knowledge of *silat* from teachers in various regions. His father had died in a fight where he was outnumbered five to one. Three of his opponents were killed and the other two were seriously injured. At the time, his father was sixty-two years old. It was a matter of great pride for their family and their village. And now he had taken his father's place and become a man held in awe and feared not just in his own village, but in several villages in his district. His father had always taught him to protect their own village. He was told not to take anything from the people in their own or nearby villages because that was where they lived and took refuge, but to take from villages further away.

He was an experienced *silat* expert. As soon as he saw the black, moving figure emerge from behind the tree heading for him, he quickly twisted his body to dodge the attack, and felt the wind of the foot that was meant to strike his head pass in front of his forehead.

Quickly he counter-attacked, swung his foot and hooked his opponent's foot just as it reached the ground, trying to topple him over. But his opponent quickly lifted his foot, evading the dangerous attack, and retreated a step backwards to the clearing. He leapt up and kicked his foot towards the chest of his opponent who caught it with his hand and retreated one more step. He kept up his onslaught, raining blows with his right and left hands, pressing and forcing his assailant to the middle of the clearing. Suddenly he stopped attacking and said, 'I'm glad you came, Dik. You are a brave man. Do you want to go on with this challenge of yours?'

'The step has been taken, Mas, I will not retreat.'

'All right, but I would like to say something to you first.'

'Go ahead.'

'Dik, you have just come into our district. If you want to make a living, do not go to our village and the other villages here. There are still plenty of other places. Be reasonable. We are all seeking a livelihood in our own way. But I have to defend this area if other people try to move in. I asked you here to tell you this.'

His opponent, who seemed younger than he was, said, 'I understand, Mas, but I cannot retreat.'

'That is a pity, you are still young. What if I asked you to join me?'

'No, Mas, I do not want to take orders from anybody.'

'That is a pity,' he said again, 'because men like us should not be enemies killing each other. We share the same fate. Are we not outcasts since the land of our forefathers was stolen from them, and from one generation to the next we have had to survive on our courage and fighting skill? Are you married?' he asked.

'No.'

'Oh, that is the reason you are not prepared to give it

more thought. Do you still want to continue this?'

Suddenly his opponent leapt to the attack; he dodged quickly and his opponent said, 'That's enough, Mas. Words will not settle this thing between us.'

And they kicked and struck at each other again. Clearly the young man was quite powerful, strong and fast. Several times he was hard pressed but his experience got him out of trouble.

He launched attack after attack; a succession of kicks, blows with his right and left hands, kicks with his body twisting, all done to gauge his adversary's vulnerability. He was pleased to see that he was not puffing. He enjoyed feeling the sweat flowing and wetting his body. After fifteen minutes of trying to penetrate each other's defence, he felt the condition of his body, his energy, speed and skill had developed to reach his peak.

Suddenly he halted his attack and stopped, standing calmly, in an attitude of readiness, his eyes locked on those of his opponent.

His opponent felt something change. It was as though their fight had reached a new, deciding phase. The young man became cautious, moving slowly, ready to defend himself or to attack, circling him slowly, and he too turned his body following the movements and steps of his opponent.

He felt calm and tranquil in himself, and his breathing was regular. Every time he inhaled he felt the strength within him increase, and with all his will he ordered that strength to flow to his legs, to the ends of his feet, to his hands right through to his fingertips and to every part of his body. He felt strong, strong, strong, and suddenly he exploded all of his strength, leaping to the attack, both feet, both hands, both fists, all moving fast. Everything felt easy and light to him and the hard, fast movements did not tire him. It was as though his hands and feet were moving of their own accord. His opponent did not waver. He skilfully dodged the first, fast rain of kicks and blows. The attacks came faster and faster, and he kept on defending and dodging them as they came, more and more rapidly. A kick got through and his opponent was forced back and stood shaking. He let go another kick and the young man fell to the ground. He leapt at his head, raised his foot, but something held him back and he lowered it to the ground.

His opponent tried to get up but fell back again. Then he opened his eyes and looked at his enemy who had defeated him.

'Why don't you finish it off?' he asked.

'You are still a young man, Dik, you can go.' He turned and walked off into the teak forest, climbed down the hill and crossed the rice fields far away from the villagers who had started work.

He knew the consequences of what he had done. It was very likely that this man would carry a grudge against him as long as he lived and would always try to avenge himself, try to kill him. The best thing he could have done was to kill the man. It wasn't as though he had never killed anyone. Since his father died he had killed three men. His father himself was said to have killed twelve men in his lifetime.

But just now when he had been about to release the death blow to his enemy's head, suddenly in his mind's eye he had seen his son still sleeping, covered up in his sarong. Since his child had grown and started school, he felt he didn't want him to take his place and follow his way of life—a life based on being the best at fighting, killing, looting, stealing, living by deeds that one day would have to be paid for with his life or imprisonment.

'I must break the red thread that has run through our lives for generations,' he said to himself.

He trembled with fear, imagining that it could have been his own son, grown up, a young man sprawled in that clearing, waiting for the death blow to his head, as his enemy had been just now. He thought of his wife, the mother of his child. And at the same time he also felt he didn't have the power to change his life. He remembered when he was wandering around pursuing knowledge of *silat* in various places, he had met all kinds of people. In some conversations there were those who said that the lot of the little man, the man who owned no land, the peasant who worked land owned by others, the unemployed in the villages, their lot could be improved if only the social order was changed and the land was distributed to those who had none. Formerly, much of the people's land had been seized by the Dutch and turned into big plantations. As a result of this many of them no longer owned any land.

When he heard words like those his heart had felt full of hope which he had held on to, but now he felt that hope would never be fulfilled.

Reaching the road to his village, he met some villagers who greeted him and he responded. But he always felt that although he was a member of their village, nevertheless he was outside the village community. He also felt worried about whether to teach his son *silat*. He was already eight years old and actually could start to learn. But if he taught his son *silat*, surely the boy would follow his footsteps, as he had followed his father's, who had followed his father's and so on. On the other hand, supposing he didn't hand down his knowledge to his son, what would he become later? They owned no land except the small plot where their house stood. Would his son be unemployed in the village? Would he become a peasant tilling the land owned by others, living in misery without hope for the rest of his days?

When he arrived home, his son had gone to school and his wife had prepared breakfast for him. She didn't ask him where he had gone when he left the house before daybreak. She never asked him where he went or what he did. She never asked where he got the money that he gave her at any time. Now and then he gave her a lot, often a little, and sometimes, for quite a long time, he gave her nothing. His wife was used to taking care that their housekeeping money lasted for as long as possible. She herself worked whenever she could, helping with the harvest in the fields, pounding rice—ah, there was not much work available in the village.

That evening, when they were eating, he said to his wife, 'I've been thinking. We can't go on living like this. We have nothing.'

His wife was silent. She did not say anything.

A month later he went to the office of the village head and registered himself, his wife and his son as candidates for transmigration out of Java.

After three months, when he had no news and the village head wasn't able to give him any, even though several families in their village and in nearby villages had already left, he went to find out for himself. A district office official whom he knew, finally told him that he had been rejected as a transmigrant for the reason that he was known as an outlaw!

He was not surprised. He had guessed as much. As he had imagined himself, for men like him there was no way out. Only if society changed could his life be changed.

He went back home. After his son got home from school, in the late afternoon he asked him to come to the deserted field near the hilltop far away from the village.

'Come on, my boy!'

And he began to teach his son *silat*.

CHAPTER TWO

Burnt to Ashes

SHE sat limply on the rattan couch on the back veranda of the house. Her hair was loose on the back of the couch and she hadn't done her sleeping kimono up properly. It was open at the top showing three-quarters of her breasts, and below, her thighs were exposed way above her knees. In her left hand she held half a glass of whisky. When she had first sunk down on the couch she had filled the glass to the brim. The first swallow had half finished it.

Safira felt the warmth of the whisky start to spread from her stomach to the other parts of her body. She began to feel more steady and not as shaky and floating, empty and cold as she had been when she first woke up. She closed her eyes and enjoyed the warmth that filled her whole body. Lying like that she made a strange picture, as if she were a portrait by an eighteenth-century Italian artist who painted fat women, full of sex appeal, like ripe fruit. Only Safira this morning looked overripe. For the past few years she had not wanted to celebrate her birthday any more, and her sharp-tongued friends said that was a sign that she had turned sixty, if not even more.

Suddenly the phone rang and, hearing the steps of her servant hurrying to answer it, without opening her eyes she said in a rather hoarse voice, 'Say I'm still in bed with a headache I've had since yesterday.'

But the servant came back and said, 'It's Noni, Ma'am. She says it's important and she says what are you doing in bed at this time of day and shouldn't you be up and starting your drinking.'

'Huuuuh,' Safira complained and grumbled, 'Noni pretends she knows everything.'

But she laughed a little then. Noni, her daughter, her only child. Their relationship as mother and daughter was close and affectionate. Noni always sided with her mother, especially in the past against the numerous fathers in succession who had occupied her mother's bed and sat on the dining-chairs or in the sitting-room.

'Hullo Noni, you are making a lot of noise early in the morning. What's the matter?' said Safira.

'Yes, you were up, weren't you, Mother, and Mbok tried to fool me.'

Safira laughed.

'Oh, so you are laughing, Mother, I'm pleased to hear it. It's a pity you can't laugh again like you used to, without drinking a glass of whisky first.'

'Ah, this morning I've only had half a glass, Noni.'

'That's what I want to remind you of, Mama. You mustn't drink a lot now, you musn't get drunk and fall asleep again. Later this morning Papa number two, Andre, is coming, isn't he?'

'Papa number two? Andre? Who is that? What does he want?' said Safira, pretending to be surprised.

'Huuuss, don't pretend to act innocent, Mama. Didn't he telegram a week ago from Brussels? He wants to come to talk about the sale of your house in Brussels. He needs your signature and your agreement and wants to discuss the division of the proceeds of the sale. Now, Mama, you don't want him to see you drunk. Don't let him think you are like that, he'll make a big fuss. It's a matter of pride, Ma!'

'Pride? What's the good of pride to me anymore, Noni? I'm too far gone.'

'Huusss, Safira, listen to me!' Noni raised her voice a little. Always between them if Noni wanted to attract her mother's attention more closely, she called her by her name, as if they were just friends. And Safira was happy that Noni did this, reminding her of the past when Noni had not yet married and they were always together, each pouring out her feelings and tribulations like two close and loving friends. She used to enjoy it in the past, provoking Noni to always call her by her name. Safira laughed, 'Yes, what is it, Noni?'

'It's like this, Ma, I'll come over in a little while and you let me get you dressed and see that you don't drink any more. Andre wants to come at twelve o'clock, which means he hopes to be invited to lunch. Isn't he crazy about Indonesian food, like all your husbands were? Also, you must have someone with you when you face Andre in case he flatters you, then you would sign anything carelessly, lose the house and your share of the money and Andre would take it all himself.'

Safira laughed and felt pleased that Noni was coming. 'Yes, you'd better come over and help me, Noni. Mbok always has to be told everything.'

'And you won't have anything more to drink, will you? Promise?' stressed Noni.

'I promise.' Safira laughed and put down the phone, walked leisurely to the small table beside the couch and in one gulp finished the whisky left in the glass.

'Come here, Mbok,' Safira called the servant. 'At twelve o'clock there's a guest coming here for lunch and Noni's coming too. Go and do the shopping and cook something nice.'

'What will I cook, Ma'am?'

'Uh, yes, what?' Safira became uncertain, and suddenly smiled.

'Oh, just wait for Noni, she'll be here soon. Let her arrange it.'

Safira went back to her bedroom, shut the door and stood in front of the large mirror above her dressing-table. Slowly she took off her kimono so that she stood naked in front of the mirror. It reflected a woman she did not know. 'Is that me?' she said to herself. She felt unhappy at what she saw.

Her body was bloated, not taut and firm as it had been ten years ago. Her stomach bulged and drooped somewhat. Her breasts were large but slack and sagging, her face was rather puffy with dark shadows under her eyes, and her hair dishevelled and dry, no longer shining with oil as it used to be. Safira put her face up close to the mirror and opened her eyes wide and felt unhappy to see the red blood vessels there, in the eyes which ten years ago had still sparkled full of lustre and thrilled the men whom she had glanced at. She pulled her cheeks that were once smooth and firm. Then she opened her mouth and drew her lips back to show her teeth. 'Eighty per cent of them are false,' she said to herself. Where was the pretty Safira, captivating men, full of passion for life, ten, twenty, thirty, forty years ago? Was this how time and age eroded a woman's beauty and appeal? What was left for her now?

Safira moved back a few steps and looked at herself in the mirror again. She took another step back. Ah, from a distance she could see traces of her body's beauty and suddenly she felt a great emptiness come over her.

She went to the bathroom beside her bedroom. She ran some hot water mixed with water from the cold tap into the bath, then turned the hot tap full on and while she waited for the bath to fill she brushed her teeth. She turned both taps off and forced herself to get into the hot water, immersing her whole body. The sting of the hot water felt sharp, burning her skin, but she restrained her impulse to leap out again because of the heat. Soon she felt a pleasant warmth enveloping her whole body. Safira closed her eyes, enjoying soaking in the hot water ... and suddenly, who knows whose hand turned the knob of her imagination, she remembered her first meeting with Andre ... in a traditional Japanese bath-house in a small town in Japan. Oh, how many years ago that was, when she was still a young woman, her husband a diplomat in the Indonesian Embassy in Tokyo, and it was her first vacation by herself out of Tokyo.

She was soaking just like this in a bath-house in a traditional Japanese hotel, where men and women bathed together in a big bath. When Safira had opened her eyes she suddenly saw before her a white man who looked at her as though he were under the spell of some power which he could not resist. And as soon as she opened her eyes, Andre said, 'You are the most beautiful woman in the world to me, and your eyes, your eyes, the bluish-green colour of your eyes, I am drowning in them.' And Safira had looked at him and said aloofly, 'Do I know you?'

'Ah, forgive me. I am Andre. I'm the Belgian Consul in Osaka. I am not married. Would you have dinner with me?'

That was the beginning of her life with Andre and the beginning of the end of her marriage to Ahmad Kesuma, the father of Noni, the only child of all her marriages. A smile lit up her face remembering how Andre pursued her to Tokyo, dissatisfied with their stolen meetings, and pressed her to marry him.

Safira felt the presence of something pleasant filling her body, remembering the years she was in love with Andre. She forgot her position as Ahmad Kesuma's wife, she forgot that she was the mother of a five-year-old daughter. She did not really know what happened when she finally gave in, and followed Andre to Singapore to his new post there, when he was transferred only six months after his first meeting with Safira.

Thinking of Ahmad Kesuma, Safira remembered the years of the revolution in Indonesia. Her father, a Dutchman, was the administrator of a sugar plantation in East Java. Her mother was Javanese. She was also an only child. When she was sixteen years old the Japanese army landed on the Island of Java. Her father had earlier disappeared into military service. When the Japanese lines conquered the whole of Java, her mother left the big plantation house and took her to the small place where her grandparents lived near Malang. During the period of the Japanese occupation she lived among her mother's people and all of her father's Dutch cultural influence quickly faded. The Japanese forbade the people to use the Dutch language. Despite this she and her mother spoke Dutch together, because her mother didn't want her to forget her father's language, as she was full of hope that he would come back for them when the war was over. Her mixing with the young people in that small place and the indoctrination she received at school made her feel that she was an Indonesian. She sang all the patriotic songs that they were taught and shouted all the political slogans they heard. That was the only way for her to be accepted by her friends. Her dark brown skin and her black hair made her no different from her other Indonesian friends from a distance. Only her more pointed nose and her bluish-green eyes revealed the secret of her mixed blood.

Her mother was very disappointed when the war ended and her husband did not come home, and when, later, war broke out between the Netherlands and the Indonesian Republic, Safira and her friends joined a Red Cross Unit. Very reluctantly her mother let her go. They moved around following the forces from one battlefield to another.

Safira smiled, remembering how she lost her virginity to a captain in an empty hospital storehouse, and then their unit was sent to Yogya. In Yogya she met an important man in the central government, a member of the team negotiating with the Dutch, a young man who had been educated in Holland, returned to Indonesia at the end of World War II and immediately joined the Government of the Republic of Indonesia.

His name was Zainul and Safira saw in him a way out of the meaningless life that awaited her if she stayed on with the Red Cross Unit. To end up having to marry a captain did not interest her at all. Zainul succeeded in appointing her as his secretary on the basis of her skill in Dutch. He also arranged for her to learn typing and compiling reports and correspondence. Safira had a natural talent for this work and in a few months she was accepted as a skilled member of the secretariat. Zainul and Safira cleverly concealed their sexual relationship, so as not to upset their other friends.

Safira wrote to her mother saying she was working in Yogya and invited her to come. After she had been there a week, her mother asked her wouldn't it be better if she married Zainul straight away?

'Ah, Mother, I don't love him,' said Safira.

'But you...!' said her mother.

'You know?'

And for the first time in her life Safira had a terrible quarrel with her mother. Safira explained to her mother that she did not want to tie herself to any man now. Conditions were unstable. No one could be relied upon and no one knew what was going to happen either.

'In that case, what do you want, Safira?' pressed her mother. 'Where will sleeping with all kinds of men, like you do, get you?'

'Mother,' said Safira, 'as an Indo woman with mixed Dutch and Indonesian blood, for women like me, life in this country is not easy. They are suspicious of me because of my Dutch blood. The colour of my eyes betrays me and betrays my brown skin and black hair. In their eyes an Indo woman is prey they must hunt, especially in a state of war like there is now. I need protection. What capital have I got to gain protection? Only my body that they enjoy. But I will not tie myself to one man now. I still want to know more about life and the world first. I want to know the world and life outside Java and I want to know about the people and life in Papa's country ...' and suddenly Safira burst into tears and sobbed to her mother, 'I want to know first, am I Indonesian or am I Dutch?'

Hearing that her mother wept, 'Oh Safira, I cannot help you find the answer to your question. Perhaps I sinned in bringing you into the world. But was it a sin to love your father? Is love a sin? We both loved you and we did not want to measure how much Dutch and Indonesian blood you have.'

'Mother, do you understand my feelings? Forgive me, Mother, but often I feel a great passion arise in me to unite myself with Indonesians and that passion brings me to sleep with them. But at other times I feel a strange call, a feeling distant from them, and I think of Papa and I want to know his people. In my work I often meet Dutch people. Sometimes I am attracted to them, but often also I get fed up and revolted looking at them, with their attitude as if they know better what's good for this country and its people than the Indonesian people do themselves. Sometimes it's as though I feel I'm only a spectator here, watching from the distance, without any feeling at all. But there are also times when I feel full of passion. I feel warm and hot, and my spirit fires my body and I feel one with them. I feel the pain of their wounds, their sorrows make my tears fall, their joys are my joys and I feel happy because of them. Why do I feel like this, Mother?'

Her mother had embraced her and said with tears rolling down her cheeks, 'God protect this innocent child of mine, give her Your mercy as she seeks her life's path ... Safira, I can only pray to God, I can only ask Him to protect you.'

What really shocked Safira was when, one day, Zainul asked her whether she would be prepared to be trained to become a spy.

'What, you want to make me into a Matahari?'

Safira was very angry. She remembered Matahari, also an Indo woman from Indonesia, who became a spy in Paris during World War I, and was finally caught and shot by the French.

'You could bring yourself to this!' she said bitterly. From then on she avoided Zainul and also broke off their secret meetings.

The second blow Safira suffered occurred when a member of the Dutch delegation approached her in Kaliurang.

'Your father was a respected Dutchman. Yes, Mr van Keerstens formerly had a very good name in the Dutch Indies. Where is your mother now? Have you heard the news about your father?'

Hopefully Safira asked, 'Is Papa still alive? Why doesn't he look for us?'

But her hopes were shattered when the Dutchman said, 'Forgive me for raising your hopes, Miss. Your father was killed during the Japanese occupation when they took him to build the railway line in Riau. The Japanese never told you? Oh, it's just terrible if they didn't.'

Safira, who had already resigned herself to the fact that her father had probably died during the Japanese occupation, was not too surprised by the news she heard. Seeing that she was still calm, the Dutchman plucked up his courage, 'Yes, Miss, your father was a great Dutch patriot. We hope his daughter will prove herself to be a great Dutch patriot, like her father.'

'What do you mean, sir?' Safira asked, rather surprised. 'You know I work with the Indonesian Republic.'

'Yes, that's really good. Our task will be easier.'

'What do you mean, our task?'

'You will go on working with the Republic, but in fact you will be working for us, the Dutch government.'

'Do you mean you want me to work as a Dutch spy?'

Hearing Safira's voice rising, the Dutchman looked at her more sharply. 'Yes,' he said, 'we hope you will carry out your duty as a patriotic Dutchwoman.'

After Zainul and now this, Safira could not control her anger any more.

'You bastard! Indonesians and Dutch are just the same, you only want to use me for your own ends,' and without her realizing it, her hand flew up in the air and slapped the Dutchman's face. And Safira ran off and left him. He had never expected her to react like that. For a long time he just stood, looking after her.

At home, she told her mother of her experience. 'They're all the same, Mother. Because I am an Indo, both the Dutch and the Indonesians think they have the right to use me as their tool. I am disgusted with all of them. From now on I am only going to think of myself. To hell with all of them! I'm on my own in this world, Mother. You can't help me and neither can Father any more.'

How her mother had tried to persuade her that one day she would be certain to meet a man who loved her, because she was Safira, a human being full of goodness and gentleness. But Safira disputed everything her mother said.

'The world is cruel, Mother,' she said, 'and it is cruellest of all to people like me, people who live between two worlds, not fully accepted by either of them. This is my fate, Mother, and I have to use all of the strength within me to protect myself.'

Her mother wept.

When finally the Dutch acknowledged the independence and sovereignty of the Republic of Indonesia, and Safira made up her mind to move to Jakarta and work in the Foreign Ministry, her mother decided to return to her parents' town. Their parting in Yogya in January 1950 was the last time Safira saw her mother, because she died a few years later when Safira was overseas.

Ahmad Kesuma, a young diplomat, fell in love with Safira the first time they met. He told her he was soon to be posted to Tokyo and his career in the diplomatic service seemed smooth and untroubled because his father was a cabinet minister. An ambassadorship awaited him at the end of his diplomatic career, and after that, who knows, a ministerial position was not impossible. Would Safira fill his life beside him, because for him it was all meaningless without her?

Safira played her cards carefully. She did not love Ahmad Kesuma, but on the other hand, his appearance and his character were pleasing enough.

'Look, if he were a bit taller he'd be handsome,' Safira

said to herself, 'and his face is not ugly. And looking to the future,' she thought, 'there can be no harm in trying with Ahmad Kesuma.' She was still young and if necessary, could always look for new opportunities.

So they were married. And then Andre came into her life via the bath-house in Japan. And after Andre ... Safira smiled. Two years in Singapore ... meeting the Indian military attaché, a virile and handsome Punjabi officer, full of sex appeal, and Safira felt as though she was suddenly attacked by a typhoon that swept her away high into the heavens. Major Khumar carried her to peaks of sexual pleasure she had never reached before, not even with Andre.

Perhaps Andre knew, but he never showed it, until Safira took Noni and left him and followed Major Khumar to New Delhi when he was transferred from Singapore because his posting there was finished. Andre chose to concede rather than face a troublesome affair that could disrupt his diplomatic career. He divorced Safira and Major Khumar married her.

At that time Nehru was still alive, and because Safira was an Indonesian and Major Khumar was one of his favourite officers, he attended their wedding. It was widely reported in the Indian press as a symbol of the close kinship between India and Indonesia. A new world full of happiness opened up before Safira. Noni whom she loved was with her, and Khumar ... for the first time in her life she felt peaceful and calm ... her restlessness disappeared.

But her heaven did not last very long. Two years later she felt Khumar change towards her. He began to insinuate that his military career seemed to have come to a halt because he had a foreign wife. They began to quarrel a lot. And Khumar became more crude towards her and increasingly sadistic in their sexual relations. This sadism had been apparent since the first time they had sex together, but it was not so crude as to upset Safira; in fact it excited her. But now it hurt her and when afterwards they had more quarrels,

Safira decided to leave Khumar. She complained to Nehru and he arranged for Khumar to support her until such time as she remarried. Khumar divorced her.

Safira and Noni returned to Indonesia. She bought a house in the Kebayoran area and tried to reorganize her life. When she was still Andre's wife, he, in the fervour of his love for her, had bought a house in Brussels in both of their names. The house was let and they shared the rent that came from it. With the money from Khumar and the rent from the Brussels house Safira was able to live quite well. But it was not long before she began to feel restless again. The meetings and relationships she had with several men in Jakarta, both Indonesians and foreigners, did not satisfy her. When the lease on the house in Brussels was up, she sent a letter to Andre telling him of her intention to stay there for a while.

For two years she was in Europe, and three times she changed her life's partner: a Frenchman, a Dutchman and an Englishman, all of whom Noni called 'Papa'. But she did not find what she was looking for. Actually, she could not explain what she was looking for in a man, or what she wanted from a man. All of this time she had always experienced men who only wanted to use her body and herself to satisfy themselves. Safira to them was only a woman's body that attracted and fired their sexual passion. No more than that. And she rebelled against this. She really wanted a man to accept her as a human being with the same rights as himself. Of them all, perhaps it was only Andre who had come closest to this attitude. Safira felt she had wronged Andre, because he had not done anything to her. But neither had Ahmad Kesuma.

'Why was Andre coming himself to discuss the sale of their house in Brussels?' suddenly this question arose in her mind. 'Couldn't this matter have been settled by letter?' Suddenly her heart pounded. She felt young again. Perhaps Andre wanted to see her again. A strong desire arose to look her best when she met him. But where was Noni? She had not arrived and she'd promised to come straight away. Then Safira bathed and cleansed herself thoroughly.

She was almost finished when Noni's voice was heard calling in the bedroom. She came in and Safira looked at her with great pleasure. She always felt like that. She had grown into a beautiful woman since she married and had two children. Noni seemed to feel none of the restlessness, confusion and anxiety that tormented her. Point! Perhaps her childish insight seeing her mother's life close up had taught her how to avoid the same fate.

'Uh, Mama, you've purposely stayed in the bath a long time to let me come and wash your hair, haven't you? You always like being spoiled. Where's the shampoo so we can get finished quickly?'

Capably Noni washed Safira's hair. Safira felt very happy. This was a mother–daughter game from the early days. And then when Safira got dressed, Noni combed her hair and said, 'Look, Mama, if you looked after your figure and dressed well, just look in the mirror, aren't you still pretty?'

And Safira looked in the mirror and felt happy. Her face was now radiant, reflecting her nice feelings and lit by Noni's love for her, and her hair, oiled by Noni, was shinier.

'How is he, Noni? Have you seen him?'

'Not yet. He only telephoned from his room when he arrived yesterday.'

'What else did he say?'

'He asked about you. Were you well and all the usual things.'

'Why don't you just talk to him, Noni? I think I'd be uncomfortable meeting him again. You know, don't you, that I just left him. By the way, how is your father now?'

'He has retired.'

'Does he still write to you?'

'From time to time. And if he comes to Jakarta he telephones and asks me out for a meal.'

'Does he ask about me?'

'Always. All the men who've known you, how can they ever forget you, Mama ... huh?' and Noni pinched her mother's cheek, teasing her.

'Hey, has Mbok organized lunch?'

'She has, Mama. It's all been taken care of.'

They were absorbed in the dressing and chattering, when suddenly Mbok came and knocked at the door and said that the guest had arrived. Safira was startled and looked quite flustered. Noni squeezed her hand to calm her. Andre turned to face them when they entered the sitting-room.

'Safira, you haven't changed at all, you are still as pretty as ever. May I ...?' he opened his arms and embraced Safira and kissed her mouth. 'Noni, my child,' and he did the same to Noni.

Andre sat next to Safira.

'How is your wife?' Safira asked.

'Ah, you didn't hear, I'm sorry, I didn't write about it. She died last year of stomach cancer.'

'Oh....' Safira didn't know what to say. 'Your children?'

'They've both left home.'

Safira felt calm seeing Andre's attitude. Noni left them and went to the kitchen with the excuse that she wanted to check the food. For a moment they looked at each other after she left them.

'Andre, why have you come? Wouldn't it have been better to let the past stay in the past? You could have written to me about the sale of the house.'

'Oh, that was just an excuse to come.'

Safira's heart thudded. 'What do you mean?'

'I wanted to see you again.'

'Andre, don't play with me.'

'It's true, Safira.'

'Now you've seen me again, what do you intend to do?'

'Ah, not now, Safira; Noni will be back any moment. When the time is right I'll tell you. What do you think of my idea of selling our house?'

'Why do you want to sell it, Andre? Do you need the money?'

'Yes, but not too urgently. I thought that with my share of the proceeds and my savings, I would buy some farming property in the south of Belgium. Soon I will be resigning from government service and life in big cities doesn't appeal to me. Unless you still need the house, Safira...?'

She laughed, 'Ah, what's the use of a house in Brussels to me, Andre? I'm not going to live in Europe for any length of time again. Andre, I've never asked your forgiveness for leaving you.'

'Hush, Safira. You don't need to ask for forgiveness. I loved you so much I accepted whatever you did. When it was for your greater happiness I bowed to it.'

'No, Andre, I wronged you; now I ask your forgiveness.'

Andre embraced her shoulders, kissed her cheek and whispered in her ear, 'Safira, Safira, you never knew how much I loved you, did you?'

A fond, warm feeling enveloped Safira's body, and she felt so moved by the extent of Andre's goodness that her eyes glistened with tears that welled up, and just then Noni came in.

'Ah, are you two getting to know each other again?' she teased.

'Noni, you arrange with Andre the documents needed for the sale of the house in Brussels. I don't understand matters like that.'

After lunch, Andre and Noni went to the public notary and returned together bringing the notary's clerk to ask for Safira's signature. Andre embraced and kissed her again after the signing was finished and promised to telephone her that evening.

Noni went home.

Safira regarded herself again in the mirror in her bedroom.

'If Andre asks ... do I want to, dare I?' she asked herself. A voice inside her whispered, 'Accept, go back to him ...

this is your last chance ... remember how old you are ...
you're more than fifty, close to sixty ... hush, you be quiet,
don't mention my age ... but you must have the courage to
face the facts ... you are old ... if Andre still loves you ...
yes, why not? But, what's the use? I am like this ... he only
remembers me when I was young ... he doesn't yet see me
as I am now ... it's useless ... it wouldn't work ... I'm worn
out too ... my fire is almost out, in my stove there only
remains dust ... ashes.... You will repeat all the failures of
your marriages and your love affairs.... This really is your
last chance.... No, no I don't want to, not because I'm
afraid, but I realize that it is impossible to resume what was
broken off so long ago in the past.... My problem is how to
tell Andre without hurting his feelings ... he is too good ...
he loves me too much.'

Safira fell asleep exhausted, thinking how to refuse Andre
later that night when he asked her to come back to him.

She woke up when the servant knocked on her door,
'Ma'am, Ma'am, there's a phone call for you.'

She poured some whisky into a glass and gulped it quickly
to calm herself down.

'Hullo, Andre...?'

'Safira....'

'Andre, Andre, ... I....'

'Safira, listen to me a moment.'

'Andre, before you say anything, listen to me first....'

'Safira, calm down, wait, listen to me first. I'm sorry I've
made you like this. On the way home from your place I
thought everything over again and I reached the conclusion
that I don't have the right to come back into your life.
Forgive me, Safira. For the sake of peace and quiet in your
life, I cannot ask you for anything. We had better not meet
again. This is goodbye, Safira....'

And Safira heard him hang up. She went on holding the
phone to her ear. Then she slowly lowered the receiver, and
for a long time she stood like that, all sorts of thoughts

invading her brain ... and she understood that Andre had only acted as he had towards her to soften her up so she would sell their house in Brussels.

'Why, why did you have to do that, Andre?' And suddenly Safira screamed, 'The same, they're all the same ... to the devil with all of them ... they only wanted to use me for their own ends.'

Safira replaced the phone. That night she drank and drank and drank until she passed out in her bed.

That's how Noni found her the next day after Mbok phoned and said she should come quickly because Madam wasn't breathing.

'Oh, my poor unfortunate mother, you never knew it was impossible for you to win in your life!' Noni wept, whispering to Safira.

CHAPTER THREE

An Empty Heart

I had just got back to the hotel from a seminar session on philosophy and technology run by UNESCO in Paris. I had had a bath and was lying on my bed feeling quite worn out after a day's sitting in the meeting room of the UNESCO building. As my thoughts were wandering, suddenly the phone by the bed rang. 'Who could this be?' I thought.

'Hullo.'

'Monsieur Mochtar Lubis?' came a woman's voice.

'Yes.'

'This is Padma,' and at once she switched to Dutch to explain that she had heard from the embassy that I was in Paris and she had to see me. 'Oh,' she said, 'there's a lot I want to talk to you about. Did you hear that I have divorced Jacques?'

Ah yes, Padma, a Madurese woman of noble birth. I remembered meeting her for the first time at the home of a friend in Jakarta in 1946. Those present that night in Jakarta, which was full of danger because of the presence of Dutch forces, consisted of a number of young men and women fighters for the Indonesian Republic that had only been proclaimed there one year previously and some foreign journalists—an American war correspondent from Associated Press, another from United Press and a French war correspondent, Jacques. An Indian Major and two British officers completed the company that night.

I was working as a reporter for Antara at the time. The

other young Indonesians worked in the Foreign Ministry, and so did Padma. The aim of holding meetings like this and inviting foreign journalists and these British officers, was for no other purpose than to brainwash them, so that they would not swallow the propaganda of the Dutch colonialists who wanted to rule Indonesia again. It was to make them understand that the Indonesian people had every right to be free like the English and the Americans were. 'You didn't want to be occupied by Hitler and his Great Germany and weren't you prepared to die to defend the freedom of your people? Well, after terrible suffering under the heel of the Dutch colonizers and then suffering again from ill treatment by the Japanese military fascists (that's what we said at the time), we've had enough. We are determined we will not be dominated again by anyone at all. The only choice for us is death or freedom. All Indonesians think that. So why did the British army allow the Dutch forces to come back into our country, eh? And why does America continue to give financial aid to the Dutch? Because of that aid the Dutch masters are able to send forces to Indonesia. Look at the Dutch uniforms, exactly like the American army: steel helmets, rifles, cannons, tanks, all made in America; even their rations are American. Have you all forgotten the promise of freedom made by the allies, freedom for all peoples?' Yes, we were very aggressive towards these people from the allied countries. Under attack like that they could not justify what had happened. Padma was one of the very aggressive ones and the most skilled at brainwashing these foreigners. She was a graduate of HBS[1] and was fluent in Dutch, English, and French, and if necessary, with some difficulty, she could also explain what she meant in German. Padma was not a pretty girl. On the contrary (forgive me, Padma), her face was unattractive, if you didn't want to say 'ugly'. But she was slim, with a good figure, enchanting; her skin was

[1]Dutch High School.

dark brown, her hair was long and black, and if she let it down it reached to her buttocks. Padma's power of attraction was in her big, round, black eyes that always sparkled, reflecting the happiness of her heart, her strong zest for life and her great femininity. Whoever looked into her eyes would feel as if drawn into them. The plainness of her face would disappear, and you would feel held in something warm and beautiful.

Another thing that would dispel her ugly face, her flat nose and wide mouth with thick lips ('thick slices of meat', her friends used to say when they were teasing her), was her skill at dancing. From time to time at meetings like that, if there were a lot of foreign guests, she would be asked to dance, accompanied by a set of simple *gamelan* instruments. And when she danced, she changed. She turned into a heavenly princess. She bewitched everybody present. One evening, accompanied only by a drum, Padma performed a Balinese dance and that night she truly bewitched us all. Looking back, I think that was when Jacques fell in love with her. I almost fell in love with her myself. But because I already had someone else, I wasn't captivated by the magic power of the look in her eyes when she performed the Balinese dance that night.

She and I were close. It was a relationship of friendship. Moreover, she was older than I was. But she always considered me as her brother. She told me all her feelings, her joys and her sorrows. In those years of struggle we felt close, and there was always a strong sense of helping each other.

A few months after that night, Padma told me that she and Jacques had fallen in love.

'I know,' I said.

'Hey, how do you know?'

'From Jacques' eyes when he looks at you and from yours when you look at him.'

'Ah, it's so obvious, is it?'

'Your eyes are windows into your feelings,' I said.

Padma laughed. 'Jacques has asked me to marry him, right away.'

'What's the hurry?'

'Because he's leaving for Indo-China immediately. The situation there is very tense too and the war against the French has started.'

'And do you want to?'

'I'm confused. I feel that we are still struggling against the Dutch. Why should I go with Jacques to Indo-China? Isn't my duty here, with all of you? Our struggle has just begun, should I really leave it? What do you think?'

'It's very difficult for me to give you any advice about this. The final decision is up to you. Clearly, if you go with Jacques, we will miss you. Your work is very valuable. You've been so active all this time. We feel strong because you are here. But who and what can oppose the call of love?' I added, teasing her.

That was our only conversation about it, the first and the last. But Padma did not go to Indo-China with Jacques. When he said goodbye to us he said he would return to Indonesia as soon as possible. But he didn't get back until the beginning of 1950. His newspaper finally let him leave Indo-China and return to Paris. He came to Jakarta to repeat his proposal to Padma. Her parents, who lived in Pamekasan, Madura, did not approve of the marriage. No one at all from her family was permitted to come to Jakarta to witness Padma's wedding. Only a small group of friends accompanied her to the civil marriage service, and the next day they flew to Paris. Every time I stopped off in Paris to finish a job we always met if she and Jacques were there. Jacques, as a journalist, often travelled to other countries. If there was a war in Africa, Central Asia or South America, then he would be there. Or if there was an important international conference on war and peace anywhere in the world, then Jacques would be sure to go. Sometimes Padma went with him, but more often she stayed in Paris. They also owned a large house two hundred miles from Paris in a beautiful, wine producing province. When Padma telephoned me that night, she and Jacques had been divorced for more than five years. But I heard from friends in Paris that apparently they had parted amicably and even after they were divorced they still met occasionally and went to the opening of a new art exhibition together or to a restaurant for a meal. After they were divorced Jacques also still arranged to send new year greetings to me in Jakarta each year.

'Will Padma go home now to Indonesia?' I had asked myself. But possibly it would be very difficult for her because during the more than thirty years since she left Indonesia, Padma had never wanted to go back and visit her homeland. We all told each other she was living very happily with Jacques.

She had also exchanged her passport for a French one and had become a true French citizen. Once I asked her why she didn't want to visit Indonesia, yet every time we met in Paris she always wanted to know what was happening there, how was Indonesia, how was the world of dance, music, literature, theatre, film, and so on. She and Jacques lived in the artistic and cultural world of Paris. They mixed with Picasso, Matisse, Jean Paul Sartre, Camus before he died colliding with a tree, with musicians, writers and journalists. Every time I wanted to meet a French cultural or artistic personality it was very easy for me to do so through Padma or Jacques. Their interest in Indonesian art and culture didn't diminish. In their house in Paris was a room full of books on Indonesia: early history and culture, the art of various regions, books on Indonesian anthropology, books ranging from the past to the present, and many other kinds. My mouth watered every time I went into that room.

In response to my asking her to come to Indonesia, Padma said frankly that it was impossible for her to ever go back. 'When I married Jacques and asked my parents' permission, they refused to give it, and I chose to sever their love, thereby, for me, severing my ties with my homeland. I could not possibly have come to Indonesia without going to see my mother and father in Pamekasan. Mother died eight years ago. Father is still alive. He is very old. If I came to Indonesia, Father would be certain to hear about it. If I didn't go to see him, and how could I when all this time he has never forgiven me for marrying Jacques without his permission, then it would hurt that old heart of his. Ah, let it be. There is no need to disturb the calm surface of the pool. I am quite content to meet and chat with you from time to time, and with our other friends from the old days if they call in to Paris. You know,' she said, 'I am very fond of you. Of all the friends in our old group, I am fondest of you. You will always listen to my troubles.'

'Ah, is this a proposal?' I said, teasing her.

'If I hadn't been in love with Jacques before I would certainly have chased and caught you,' she said in response to my teasing, 'but I knew you already had someone else. How is your dear wife? Why didn't you bring her this time?'

Thus Padma always controlled herself, showing on the outside as a strong person. But I knew her. I could see that she suffered from breaking off with her parents. But she had her self-esteem and pride. So did her father and mother. Their aristocratic Madurese blood flowed strongly in them. Neither side could show a soft heart and be reconciled again. Yet before this Padma had often talked to me about her parents and about how she felt very close to them. But Padma was a strong individual. She restrained all this.

I felt a great deal of sympathy towards her now that she was old in a far-away country and alone in this big city, although she was not a foreigner here. As with everything she did, always doing her utmost and giving her whole self, so too she had made herself one hundred per cent French. The only thing she couldn't change was her appearance as a person born an Indonesian.

I used to like teasing her, saying that she had become a dark-skinned Frenchwoman.

'I have to be like this, Mochtar,' she said. 'From when my brothers and sisters and I were small my father always taught us that if you do something, you do it as well as you can, with all your body and soul. I give myself completely to anything I do.'

'Yes, I heard you were divorced and I was very surprised, but I didn't have the courage to write and ask you about it. As it happens I have nothing on tonight. If you like, I'll come over and let's have dinner together. You'll know a good restaurant.'

'Oh, you are always so nice, you never change. Come on over.' Her voice sounded very happy.

'I'll be there in half an hour.'

'I'll be waiting.'

I got dressed and found a taxi straight away outside the hotel. I gave the driver Padma's address.

When I arrived at her apartment (in a street considered as a place where prominent people lived in Paris) and knocked on her door, from inside she was already calling my name. Then the door opened and she hugged me tight, putting her head on my chest and I saw her restraining her tears with difficulty. It was more than five years since I had seen her. I had been in Paris several times during this period but she had been away. How quickly she had aged since Jacques had left her. Her cheeks were wrinkled and could not be concealed by her powder and thick make-up. Yes, Padma was at least sixty-two or -three. She no longer guarded the slimness of the dancer's body of her youth. Now she was fat, and moved heavily, not nimbly as she used to.

'Oh, you never get any older,' she said, raising her head to look at me, 'whereas I look old now. I've started getting rheumatics in my knees, and if it's cold they start hurting. Ah well, that's life.'

She took me to the sitting-room. 'We'll have some tea first before we go and have dinner,' she said, and we quarrelled a bit about who was going to pay. I said loudly that I was the one who would pay, and she said loudly that she should pay because I was her guest. I was the one who had come to Paris.

'Yes,' I argued, 'but I'm the one who invited you to dinner.'

'Nonsense,' she said, 'don't argue any more. Stop it before I get angry.'

'Oh,' I said giving in. 'I haven't come here to fight with you,' and I laughed.

'I know,' she said, 'you Eastern men have your male pride and feel small and humble if the woman pays. Why is that so? Aren't men and women the same, as human beings? The one is no more or no less than the other. Isn't that your view too?'

'You know it is,' I said.

We laughed.

'Hey, my friend,' she said, 'don't feel uncomfortable because you gave in to me. It's a practical matter too. You don't have any spare money, only what you get daily from UNESCO, I know. And at least Jacques, when we separated, wasn't mean. On the contrary, he gave me far more than he had to. He handed over the house and land in the country to me. I get the rent from them. He gave me this apartment. And he put a sum of money in the bank in my name and the interest added to the rent from the country house gives me more than enough income for a good life in Paris. Do you understand?'

'Padma, haven't I already given in?'

'This is one of the things I wanted to talk to you about,' Padma said, taking me to the studio that was full of books. 'You know, don't you, about our collection of books on Indonesia. Now Jacques isn't here any more and I am old. I want to hand these books over to Indonesia but I don't know to whom, or to what institution. I don't want them to get disorganized and lost in confusion, because we purposely collected them, because of our love for, and great interest in, Indonesia. I want these books to be taken to Indonesia and made use of there. So does Jacques. Now, who would it be best to hand them over to?'

'Hm,' I said, 'they could be given to the Central Museum library in Jakarta, or to the library of the University of Indonesia or to another university, or to LIPI,[1] it just remains to choose.'

'But which one would you guarantee would not waste the collection, and would look after it as well as possible?'

'Ha, that is another problem,' I said. 'I wouldn't dare to guarantee anyone or anything in Indonesia now.'

'Huh, is it so bad there?' she asked.

As we dined at the restaurant Padma talked excitedly about the latest French film, a cartoon, something like the story of Tarzan, called 'Tarzoon', but it was porno and very funny.

'You should see it,' she said, 'if you like I'll go with you. It's really funny.' She talked about the sensation of the fight for Picasso's estate which comprised hundreds of his paintings, she talked about French politics—'Ah, Giscard d'Estaing won't be re-elected—the French people are bored with him. There are disadvantages too, you know, in making the president's term of office up to seven years as it is here. It's too long. The people get bored and want to see a new face as their president on television. They want to see change. French politics will move to the left, just you see, and if the shift is large enough then it will influence politics in Western Europe.'

Later, we strolled along the Champs-Elysées. The air was very fresh, the streets were full, and the cafés were packed. She didn't want me to take her by taxi, but asked me to walk her home. 'I would be lazy and go by taxi if I had to go home

[1] Lembaga Ilmu Pengetahuan Indonesia (Indonesian Institute of Sciences).

by myself, especially tonight. But you are here. Let's just walk home,' she asked. She went on talking. Some of her stories were strange, interesting, full of information and sometimes funny. But I felt she was talking a lot so she could not hear the voice of her heart, the hammering of her feelings, the moaning of her spirit. To quieten something that was asking to come out of her.

When we arrived at her apartment she invited me in.

'Let's have some coffee before you go back to the hotel,' she asked.

After we had the coffee, I stood up to say goodbye and embraced her, kissed her goodnight on the cheeks and promised to telephone her about going to see the French porno cartoon or not.

As I was leaving, I said to her in a gentle voice, 'Padma, can I help you with something?'

She looked at me quickly, her eyes looking closely at mine and suddenly she stepped up and hugged me, holding her body to mine, and sobbed, 'How kind you are, old friend, but you can't help me—no one at all can help me—it's all too late. For years and years my heart has been empty, empty and cold.'

'Why, Padma? I and your friends in Indonesia thought you two were very happy all this time. We were very surprised to hear you were divorced. Jacques seemed to love you so much.'

'Life likes to give the unexpected. Jacques still keeps saying that he still loves me even now when we are divorced. I'm the one who asked for the divorce, not him.... I'll tell you now; two years after we were in Paris Jacques fell in love with another woman. I was surprised, but here that sort of thing is common and a wife is expected to understand and to have no objections. Jacques even introduced her to me, and she was not the first, but replaced someone else. What I could not accept at all, and perhaps this is because of my failure to become one hundred per cent French—the remains of my Indonesianness are apparently still inside me—was proved when Jacques got involved with a ... man. Imagine, a man! I never thought that Jacques was bisexual.... He didn't deceive me, he was frank about it all, and that happened in our third year in Paris.... Since then I have been alone, my heart has been empty, and I never wanted to sleep with Jacques again.'

'Padma, why didn't you leave him—you were still young—and go back to Indonesia?'

'It was impossible, and going back to my parents and admitting they were right? Don't I have my pride, and my own dignity? Wasn't that the right attitude? Tell me, what do you think?'

What could I say to her ... that in my opinion she had held on to her pride and her dignity too much in opposing her parents, that her pride was not appropriate, and had blinded her to other possibilities in her life which may have saved her from living with an empty heart for so long? That supposing before, years and years ago, she had been able to humble herself and had the courage to admit the failure of her marriage to Jacques, she could still have opened the door to happiness in life?

But I knew I could not tell her what I was really thinking. I knew she would grow more lonely and her heart would become more empty if I told her the truth.

'You were right, Padma; you were right,' I said.

She raised her head and looked at me and the light in her eyes searched as if a person about to drown was groping for a place to hang on to. I kissed her cheek and whispered again to her, 'You were right, Padma,' and quickly opened the door, hurried out and went back to my hotel.

And in the street, suddenly I stopped walking, startled because I realized that in my heart I was still saying, 'You were right, Padma; you were right, Padma,' as though I wanted to send a message to strengthen her heart in the long emptiness of her life. I felt deep sorrow seize my heart.

CHAPTER FOUR

The Hero

WHEN I was still held under arrest by the Soekarno regime in the Military Detention Centre in Budi Utomo Street, Jakarta, I had heard his name and stories of his heroism; Major Lintang, a courageous Permesta[1] forces leader, a slippery and skilful guerrilla war leader. I heard the story from some members of Permesta who were detained at the same place. They said that after the Central Government forces landed in Minahasa, and the Permesta forces retreated to the mountains, Major Lintang took his forces to the area around the lake.

There he succeeded in holding out for almost two years, and every time the Central Government forces tried to penetrate they were always driven back by Major Lintang. There was something unique about his force, they told me, and that was his women's squad. It consisted of young women between the ages of eighteen and twenty-five. And they really took part in the fighting, they were not there to be diversions for the men. 'Lord, you wouldn't want to try and fool around with them or you'd be beaten up by their commander, Lieutenant Nita. Oh, she was fierce, not scared of anyone at all. She was a good shot with a pistol and rifle, she could use a bayonet, do unarmed combat and she had even more endurance for walking or running, or going up and down mountains, than the men. And surprisingly she was still a woman, delightful, but you wouldn't want to try

[1]'Permesta' is an acronym from 'Persatuan Semesta' which means 'Total Struggle'.

anything. Lots of mates who did try had their ears boxed and were kicked by her. She also watched over her followers closely. In short, no one dared to annoy that squad of females. Once a new recruit came and tried to pester her women. Lieutenant Nita immediately dragged him away and kicked him mercilessly with her raider boots. He passed out.' And they laughed, remembering the incident that was so funny in their eyes.

'If the major had not been shot dead in a battle against the Central Government forces, there's no certainty that they would have been able to take the whole of Minahasa at that time,' they said. 'Oh, if only Pak Lintang had come out on top, it would have been terrific. He was a hero.'

I heard this story in the sixties and then I was transferred to various other detention centres. Then the abortive Gestapu/PKI[1] rebellion broke out, and we political prisoners of the Soekarno regime were released. I was busy with new things, often working abroad, and I forgot all about the story of Major Lintang's heroism.

From the beginning, that young woman really enjoyed coming to play tennis at the courts where we played, and I liked her. She was nice. She was cheerful, and was always joking and laughing. She was almost pretty but her lips were too straight, giving a kind of sternness to her face which only disappeared and made her look attractive if she smiled or laughed. But if her expression was just normal, then her lips changed her appearance. It was as though there were two people inside her with opposing personalities. One was stern and silent, while the other was gentle, cheerful and attractive. She had big, round, dark brown eyes and strong white teeth. And she played tennis aggressively, like a man. Usually she didn't defend but always attacked. She didn't wait for the ball to come to her, but went on the attack, swinging her arm

---

"'Gestapu' is a rather arbitrary abbreviation for 'Gerakan September Tiga Puluh', which means 'September 30 Movement'. 'PKI' is the abbreviation for 'Partai Kommunis Indonesia' (Communist Party of Indonesia).

right back and hitting it powerfully when she swung her racket in her right hand drive. Her backhand was also attacking, hitting fast and hard. She always moved on the court as if she had too much energy to use up and expend, and if she could not, it would explode inside her.

I enjoyed playing with her, both as her opponent and her partner. When we played mixed doubles, no other pair could beat us, because my style of play was like hers. I was happier attacking and hitting the ball with full force than defending. She wasn't so keen on playing the volley, and because of that, I played on the net if we were partners, and she took the back court.

A few months after she started playing with our club she was coming regularly and our relationship was just as fellow club members who enjoyed playing together. It was only gradually that she began talking about herself. The first thing she told me was that she was the niece of a very old, close friend of mine.

'Oh, Tina,' I said, 'why didn't you say so in the first place? I'll bet you've known from the beginning who I am.'

'Of course,' she said, 'when I was at high school I had to read your books.'

'Why didn't you tell me you are his niece?'

'Ah, I was embarrassed that you would think I wanted to be familiar and was asking you to take notice of me.'

'I'd be happy for you to feel close to me. Your uncle is like my brother. From now on don't be embarrassed or shy again, all right?'

From then on she did become closer to me. She started telling me about a few of her experiences. She told me especially how she did not like Aziz, a member of our club, a young married man, who was never happy unless he and his partner won every time they played. He also considered himself to be a he-man who was irresistible to all women, young and old.

'I get angry when I see him with his male conceit,' said

Tina. 'He has tried to hold me and caress my shoulders. Once he pretended he was joking. I was annoyed, eh, disgusted by his behaviour.'

'Do you want me to talk to him and give him a bit of advice?' I asked.

'Ah, don't bother. Let me handle it myself,' she said.

In the following weeks I certainly noticed Aziz becoming more aggressive towards Tina. Of course men are usually like that. If the woman they chase ignores them, their desire to conquer her increases.

Every year, a week before 17 August, we usually organized a competition between club members. There were men's and women's singles and doubles and mixed doubles. This time Tina asked me to be her partner. It proved that in the final, our pair faced Aziz and Ani, a friend of Tina's. When the final was about to start, Tina was very keen. Her eyes flashed with the spirit of battle.

'Now let's change our tactics,' she said to me. 'You look after the back court, and I'll go on the net.'

I was rather surprised because usually she didn't like playing on the net. Especially since Aziz was a skilful volley player and always played there.

Aziz and Ani were strong. Ani was very good at the lob shot. She always hit her lobs very high and way back close to the line and was very clever at placing them wherever she liked. Ani's lob shot was her very powerful defence stroke. However hard a forehand drive was hit to her left or right, she could lob it back well with her forehand or backhand.

We won the first set 6–4 with great difficulty. In the second set Aziz played more aggressively. He was like a panther on the net attacking every ball that came by. They were ahead 3–1. It was my turn to serve.

Tina stood near the net, and so did Aziz. Now, I don't want to make any propaganda for my service, but it was renowned as the hardest in my club. But in this match Ani was lucky, fortune and fate were with her. She worried me because however hard I hit my services to her, most of them she was able to lob back, high, and right near the back line.

'Try this one, Ani,' I said to myself as I threw the ball high above my head, swung my racket back and with full force hit it right on the ball. My service flew at a speed of 80 km an hour or more, heading for Ani's backhand. It's true she had trouble lobbing it back as usual. But she managed to do it anyway and the ball passed over the net in front of Aziz, destined to be easily taken up by Tina. Tina chased the ball, running hard and getting ready to smash, her racket in the correct position, and Aziz moved back a few steps, still trying to defend. I have to confess he had guts. Tina swung the racket and hit the ball with all her strength and suddenly we were all startled to hear Aziz cry out. In the blink of an eye he fell to the ground, his racket flew out of his hand and he struggled and floundered like a chicken that had just had its head chopped off. He held his groin, and suddenly he was silent. Tina's smash, with the speed of a bullet, had apparently hit his genitals. I ran and jumped over the net and other friends came over. Aziz had fainted and his face was pale.

'Ladies,' I said, 'please move back, don't look at the poor fellow. I want to examine him to see whether … ahem … there's any damage.' They couldn't control themselves and choked with laughter, but none of them would turn away. 'It's their own risk in that case,' I said, and I squatted down and undid Aziz's shorts.... Ah, fortunately there was no bleeding, only terrible shock from the blow of the ball. I did up his shorts again.

Another woman came and brought a thermos full of iced water and with a small towel she wiped Aziz's face and head. A few minutes later he opened his eyes and groaned with pain. His hands went back to protect his groin. We helped him stand up and he tottered to a bench, moaning in pain with every step he took. After he sat down he leant back and closed his eyes. When he had rested like that for five minutes we took him to his car. Luckily he had brought his driver, and Aziz went home.

When the umpire declared us the winners, I shook hands with Tina and she grasped my hand tightly and winked at me, and then she hugged Ani and kissed her on both cheeks. My suspicions grew, especially when I remembered how fierce the expression in Tina's eyes was when she stood at the net looking at Aziz rolling around on the ground. Something funny, which I did not understand yet, had happened.

Later, when we were eating noodles at the canteen, the loser treating the winners, and the three of us, Tina, Ani and I, were sitting together, what had happened still disturbed me. No one blamed Tina. In a match, what happened to Aziz was a risk you took. If you were game to stand at the net, then you had to be game to be hit by the ball.

While we were eating I whispered to Ani and Tina, 'Hey, you two are very dangerous women, I've just discovered. You look very sweet, but you can be killers,' I teased them.

They looked at me, then at each other, and I added, 'It's not that I object to Aziz being taught a lesson!'

'So, you know?' Tina asked suddenly with a smile.

'Am I not a reporter and a Sherlock Holmes at the same time? You set it up cleverly. Isn't Ani a lob expert? And Tina, who rarely plays on the net, suddenly plays there. And Ani gives a lob that is so gentle and soft right in line with Aziz and Tina is ready and waiting ... you two are terrible!'

They both looked at me and then laughed. 'You'll keep it a secret, won't you; don't tell the others.'

'I promise. If the others found out, they would surely all be frightened to play against you. They'd be more or less facing the risk of becoming impotent for three months at least.'

They giggled.

Not long after that I had an assignment to go to Sulawesi to write about a Toraja burial ceremony. The dead man was a king and it might have been the last chance to witness such an infrequent and wonderful ceremony. A burial ceremony according to Toraja custom, especially for one of the aristocracy, costs a great deal of money, you know. I met an old friend there who now held office as a *bupati* in Minahasa. He invited me to come to his district.

'Come on, you've never seen North Sulawesi, have you, and all this time you have promised you would come but never have,' he said. 'Stay at our house. Sofia, my wife, would like to see you again, too.'

So after the programme in Toraja was concluded, we went back together to Ujung Pandang and from there flew to Menado. I was pleased to have a *bupati* as a host and guide. I wanted to collect as much information as possible about the former Permesta revolt against the Soekarno regime. And suddenly I remembered again the story told by the Permesta men in the Military Detention Centre in Budi Utomo Street. I wanted to know more about Major Lintang, the hero. I told Sofia.

'Oh, there are many of his ex-followers here. And you know he had a child, a son. He lives in a village near Menado.'

So Sofia took me around and introduced me to the former members of the Permesta forces. Those whom I met had become farmers. But not just any farmers, they were clove farmers. They were very proud of their experience in opposing the Soekarno regime. One man said that the steps taken by Permesta and the PRRI[1] against the Soekarno regime and the Indonesian Communist Party had proved to be right. In the end, hadn't Soeharto and his allies also been forced to confront the Communists and attack them?

'If they had followed us before,' he said, 'it would not have been necessary to wait for Indonesia to reach the brink of bankruptcy. Oh, Major Lintang? He was a terrific com-

[1] Pemerintahan Revolusioner Republik Indonesia (Revolutionary Government of the Republic of Indonesia).

mander,' he said, speaking full of spirit. 'He defied death. He wasn't at all frightened of dying. In every battle he led the attack, and if we retreated he was the last to leave. And he really took care of his followers ... the wounded, the sick, our food, our clothing, our quarters. He looked after everything. If he hadn't been killed there's no certainty what the outcome of the war against the Soekarno regime would have been.'

'I heard that the battle that killed Lintang was the fiercest of all, is that true?'

'Oh yes, sir. Our troops were ready to ambush a convoy, the road had been mined, the first armoured car was hit by a mine and the battle broke out. Apparently the Central Government Force was larger than expected and we had to retreat. Lintang ordered his troops back, and he, with two units, covered our retreat. Those who stayed back were almost all wiped out. The only one who survived and rejoined us was the commander of our women's squad. She was the one who brought the news that Lintang had been killed.

'After the Central Government forces left, we went back that afternoon to get the bodies of our friends and Major Lintang. Oh, his body was mutilated. It was almost severed below his stomach from Bren gun fire. I remember it well. I was the one who picked his body up.'

Sofia also introduced me to some members of the Permesta women's squad. I could not imagine that these women, who had married, had children and become housewives, had formerly wandered about in the jungles of Minahasa fighting a guerrilla war, suffering and dying just the same as the men. They talked about their commander, Nita.

'Oh, Nita was special, indeed she was on a par with Lintang. She was incredibly brave. Why she was never hit by bullets is quite amazing. Because when she was in battle she would not lie down but she stood straight up and fired her Bren. Oh she was strong, even stronger than many of the men. We were all surprised by that, because in the beginning she was like us. Even when she first started to be trained to hold a rifle, she shut her eyes, like we did, when she fired.'

'When did she change like that?'

'Oh, I don't remember any more, sir. It seemed to be sudden. I remember the time we ambushed a force of Central Government scouts. When the moment to attack arrived, Nita stood up and opened fire on them. It all happened very quickly. The whole force was wiped out. She was no less of a hero than Lintang, but because she was a woman, not many people talked about her like they did about him. Isn't that unfair?'

When I asked whether she knew where Nita was now, she said no one knew. Neither did Sofia nor my friend the *bupati*. According to reports, she left Minahasa after the agreement was reached between General Nasution and General Kawilarang and Colonel Ventje Samual.

The day before I left to go back to Jakarta, Sofia took me to the village where Major Lintang's child lived. Apparently he had been brought up by Major Lintang's parents. They were both still alive and their Indonesian was mixed with Dutch.

'Please sit down, sir and madam,' said Major Lintang's father. I told him of my wish to see the major's son.

'Oh, he's not at home. He's gone to Menado with his friends.'

'Is he big now?' I asked.

'Oh yes, and he's handsome like his late father,' they said, proud of their grandson.

'Is his mother here?'

'Oh no, his mother died after he was born. You know, in war time there's no nursing and medicines. We raised him. It was funny, you know, sir, when he was first brought here ... who brought him, Papi?'

'Nita,' her husband reminded her.

'Yes, Nita. And Nita said, "This is Major Lintang's baby;

his mother died after he was born." At first we didn't believe her. We knew his wife was in Menado with their two children. But it was war time, wasn't it, and possibly Lintang had a new woman in the jungle and being married was not a problem. At first we were reluctant to accept the baby, but Nita said, "Look at his face. Isn't that Lintang's face?" Ah, it was true, and now we feel grateful that we accepted him. Oh, if you saw him, sir, he's exactly like his father. God really sent him to replace our lost son.'

It certainly looked as though Lintang's mother and father were very delighted with their grandson. He was a good child, conscientious with his studies, not too naughty, and a keen church-goer.

'We've brought him up well,' said Major Lintang's father.

The next day I thanked and farewelled Sofia and her husband and returned to Jakarta.

When I went back to play tennis again after returning from Menado, my friends asked me to tell them about Toraja Land. And then when it was our turn to sit off—Tina and I had just played—I told her that I had also gone to Menado, and about my trip to Minahasa and the stories I had heard about the hero Major Lintang, and a heroine, Lieutenant Nita.

'Goodness, the stories about her are no less terrific than those about Lintang. An unknown Permesta heroine. I tried to find her there, but no one knows where Nita is now.'

Suddenly I saw Tina's expression change, her lips straightened and she seemed miles away, alone with her thoughts.

'Did you see Major Lintang's child?' her voice was rather shaky.

'Ah no. I looked for him but only met Major Lintang's father and mother. They seem to love the child very much. They said he looks just like his father. I met many people who still talk about the two heroes, Lintang and Nita.'

'Heroes?' said Tina, and her voice shook and her eyes flashed with the fire of anger. 'Do you know who the mother of the hero Lintang's child is? It's me. I am Nita. And why

did I get pregnant with his child? Because one day he raped
me. And why do people think Nita was a brave heroine, not
afraid of death? Because when I knew I was pregnant, I
wanted to die, because I did not want to have that child, the
result of the rape of my body. But no bullets would hit me.
And then when that terrible battle against the Central
Government forces took place and Lintang stayed back with
two units to cover the retreat, I was near him and he died,
not because of enemy fire ... I killed him....'

I looked at her with shock. She didn't see me, she was
gazing far away to somewhere or other, and for her the
tennis court and her friends playing did not exist.

'I shot him deliberately with my Bren, below his stomach
and destroyed his manhood that had ravaged me. In my eyes
he was a traitor who betrayed his own followers. And when
my stomach swelled, I took myself off to an isolated village,
and after the baby was born, and I was strong enough to
travel again, I took him to Lintang's parents. I left Minahasa
and changed my name to Tina.'

And I remembered how angry she was with Aziz, who
always tried to force himself on her.

'And now that you know, are you revolted to look at me?'
she asked.

I held her hand. 'No, Tina,' I said, 'no man can be your
judge. You must find peace in your own heart. That terrible
thing happened a long time ago. Let it stay buried in the
past. I love you even more, knowing how dreadful your life
has been. I understand your feelings. But don't live the rest
of your life with hate in your heart. Life holds all sorts of
possibilities, some ugly, but also some that are beautiful.'

'For me too?' she asked in a small voice.

'Especially for you. How old are you? Thirty?'

Tina nodded.

'Heavens, life is still waiting for you.'

'Is that true? That is a question I always ask myself,' and
her gaze was miles away, who knows where.

What else could I say to her?

CHAPTER FIVE

Money, Money, Money, Only Money

Boк—his full name was Tan Siu Bok—leant back in the easy chair. He still felt very weak and tired as the result of a terrible asthma attack. He always had one if the temperature fell below 20 degrees Celsius. If he didn't quickly put on a warm jacket and light the heater, an attack would come on suddenly. For more than ten years he had suffered like this. Yet when he had lived in Indonesia he had never been troubled with asthma. That was surprising. Maybe only if he went home again to Indonesia would it get better or lessen. If it went on like this, it would take him to his grave. Bok felt sure of this. But how could he go home to Indonesia? His passport had been replaced by a Dutch one. He'd become a Dutch citizen and given up his Indonesian citizenship. Of course there was still his family, two uncles and a cousin in Surabaya, but they couldn't help him. Since he left Indonesia when President Soekarno broke off relations with Holland and seized all Dutch property in Indonesia, he had moved around to various West European countries looking for a suitable place to live, but none of them satisfied him.

He was fortunate, like a lot of his friends were, in being able to leave Indonesia with most of his wealth. His father had certainly been right, but neither he nor Bok's mother lived long enough to know how astute he was because they died long before President Soekarno severed relations with Holland. They had transferred their wealth in the form of large amounts of money, gold and jewellery, to Holland. His father had owned a sugar-cane plantation and a sugar factory in Central Java.

When Indonesia was occupied by the Japanese they had been safe because they were willing to cooperate with Japan. The plantation sugar factory worked for Japan, handed over all the produce to the Japanese army, and received payment in worthless Japanese army paper money. But his father had been clever. With the paper money he bought gold, jewellery, a house and land. And when Japan surrendered, his wealth did not decrease, it grew. After the war of independence, his father sold the house and land and sent the proceeds together with the gold and jewellery to be kept in a bank in Amsterdam. He also bought a house in The Hague.

His father had looked far ahead to the future.

'Bok,' his father had said to Bok and his mother, 'there are only the three of us left in this world. My other relatives are supporting themselves. They don't need anything. I have told them to transfer some of their wealth abroad, because the future is unsure for people like us. The native Indonesians don't trust us. They are jealous of our wealth. They don't believe that people of Chinese descent could love this country as much as they do. They only see us as visitors whose sole aim is to amass wealth here, while our hearts and loyalty are still bound to China. They don't want to acknowledge that our ancestors took part in opening up and developing this country, or how many of them were brought here formerly by the Dutch in tens of thousands to work as coolies, carpenters, ironworkers, stonemasons, building roads and bridges, and working in the plantations and mines. And how our ancestors developed business in this country! They lived frugally, eating rice porridge morning, noon and night, gathering capital. Many of them never enjoyed the small amount they did succeed in gathering because they left it to their children, to go on being added to, so that the family could finally make some progress. Ah, believe me, Bok, this is what they will not and cannot see. Neither do they want to acknowledge that many of Chinese descent like us took part in the struggle for Indonesian independence in the Dutch colonial period. They forget all this. We will always be the target for the anger of the Indonesian people and also if necessary, the target or scapegoat for those who hold power here. If there is anything wrong it will always be the fault of the Chinese again. So we must always be prepared in case we have to leave this country at any time. Do not think, Bok, that I would be happy doing this. I love this land. My mother and father were born here. Your grandmother owned a part of Indonesia, but that does not make us accepted by Indonesian society. This country has given a good life to our forefathers and to us. Don't forget that, Bok. Whatever happens, you must always love this country. Even if we are forced to leave one day, don't forget, Bok. This country has given life to us.'

'But do you know what they say about us Chinese, Father?' Bok said.

Bok had Indonesian friends who went to school with him in Holland. Only Bok did not finish his schooling because after he had been studying for three years at university in Holland his father called him home to help him in the business.

'That's enough, Bok. You are already good at Dutch, English, French and German, you know all kinds of things and that's enough for people like us. It's time for you to learn to be a businessman now.'

And Bok, who really wanted to continue his schooling and finish his studies as a lawyer with his other Indonesian friends, obeyed and followed his parents' wishes. It did not occur to him to argue with them.

But he continued his friendly relationship with the Indonesians with whom he had studied in Holland, after they returned to Indonesia. They were open with him when he was with them. Because of that Bok knew well their views on the Chinese in Indonesia.

'Look, Bok,' they said to him, 'if the people of Chinese

descent were all like you and felt themselves really children of this country, then there would be no problem, would there? But look at the facts, the ones like you can be counted on the fingers. And don't the Dutch have a proverb, "one swallow does not make a summer"? You know there are Chinese here who have lived in this country from one generation to another, but still can't speak Indonesian. Those are the full-blooded Chinese, living in closed groups and marrying among themselves. If they are men, they are allowed to marry Indonesian women, but if an Indonesian man wants to marry a Chinese woman, even though she is willing, her parents will strongly forbid it. You all live in your own world, maintaining Chinese language and culture, not wanting to join in Indonesian society. Look, in economic life, because the Dutch were frightened in case the economy of the indigenous Indonesians became strong, it was the Chinese who were given the opportunity to become the middle class. You control middle and small businesses. You are happy holding that position. You help each other, and if competition from native Indonesians arises, you join together to destroy it. In education you build your own schools. When are you going to integrate with the Indonesian people, if you still want to stand apart and hang on to the cultural characteristics of your ancestors and your homeland here?'

Bok frankly acknowledged that the views of the Indonesians were correct. And he told them to his father. And his father fell silent.

'This is the tragedy of our race here, Bok,' his father said, 'perhaps it's all too late. I am convinced that the main fault is ours, because we were the newcomers, but did not really try to integrate with the local people.'

'Yet our ancestors who first came here understood like we do now. But when we all began to understand and be aware, possibly it was already too late, because the native Indonesians had their own views and attitudes towards us, based on our mistakes all this time.'

'But shouldn't someone take the first step?' said his father.

'Who's it going to be?'

Father and son looked at each other, lost for ideas, unable to find an answer. Bok said to his father that they, as members of the wealthiest class in the Chinese group, could not possibly do it, because they were the ones most suspected and mistrusted by the native society.

'My friends are Indonesians,' Bok said to his father, 'they only trust me as one individual to another, but if things are raised to a political level, they tell me frankly that in their eyes I am only a Dutch tool to block the native people from getting a strong economic position.'

After his father, and later his mother, died, Bok lived alone in their big house in the sugar factory complex and carried on his father's work.

And then when Soekarno decreed that the Chinese were forbidden to engage in business or live in the villages, which was then followed by the seizure of all Dutch businesses and wealth in Indonesia, Bok felt that he had to carry out his father's wishes and leave Indonesia and look after their wealth in Holland.

He appointed a manager to look after the cane plantation and sugar factory and left for Holland. When he was about to leave he wrote a letter to Reni, an Indonesian girl-friend of his who often came with his friends to play tennis at the sugar factory tennis court. Reni was the daughter of a retired *bupati*. They were quite close. And every time Bok opened his heart to listen to what it was saying, he had to confess that his feelings towards Reni were more than those of ordinary friendship. And he was convinced that she felt the same way towards him. But he did not have the courage to listen to the words of his heart. In the letter, he wrote that he regretted not saying goodbye to Reni, because he knew he would not have had the courage to say what was in his heart if he saw her in person. He was also frightened in case he was able to pluck up the courage to say what he wanted to, because he did not dare to shoulder the responsibility.

'Reni, I am leaving Indonesia, as I think, for ever, because I feel there is no place for me in this country that I love. Look at what has happened to the people of my race! How I wish the situation was not pushing me to go, because I would be happier here, close to you. I will not like it wherever I go. I pray that you will find happiness in your life and think of me sometimes.' And since he had left Indonesia, he had completely broken off all contact.

After he arrived in Holland, with the aid of his father's friends who had previously moved there, he carefully invested the capital his father had transferred. It was guaranteed, and the interest enabled him to live like a rich man, without doing any work at all. The first years in Europe were quite absorbing. He rented an apartment in Paris, and with his Chinese friends, many of whom had moved to the Netherlands and also had enough capital, he filled in his time enjoying himself. They visited various countries in Europe—Germany, Switzerland, Italy, Spain, England, Portugal, Ireland, Scandinavia—they went to North Africa, to America, Canada, Mexico. They had no trouble replacing the girl-friends who accompanied them; Dutch, French, German, Italian, English, Spanish, Portuguese and Scandinavian girls. But after a few years Bok felt bored living like that, and without realizing it, from year to year he was drinking more. If he felt lonely, he drank; if he felt fed up, he drank. If he went out in a crowd with his friends, he drank, and if he was with a woman, he drank.

After five years in Holland he obtained Dutch citizenship and cut his final tie with Indonesia. On that day he invited his friends to drink until they got drunk, as he said, to celebrate the day he became a Dutch citizen. But in his heart he knew he was drinking till he was drunk to hide the sorrow in his heart, the loss of his homeland in this world where he was born.

'Poor Bok,' he still managed to say to himself, when he started drinking. Later he was often sick because his body had been weakened as a result of too much alcohol. He grew thin and lost his appetite. And more and more often he thought of the land of his birth, Indonesia. He remembered the hot Indonesian climate and the cool freshness in the mountains. He felt a great longing for the various Indonesian foods he had eaten since he was a child. Although there were many restaurants in Holland that served Indonesian food, Bok felt that none of them had the genuine taste of Indonesian cooking. He also longed to taste Indonesian fruits like mango, *duku*, *manggis*, *jambu*, *salak* and durian ... yes, durian.

'I am close to death,' Bok said to himself at the times his longing for Indonesia came to attack him like this. And more unfortunate again he felt, he began to long for Reni again. Her face, which had been as if wiped from his memory, now began to appear in his mind again. And every time her face appeared it was brighter and more clearly imagined in his memory.

'I really am close to death,' Bok thought.

His friends advised him that it would be best if he got married. They said if he had a wife she could look after him and care for him. But Bok was not at all interested in getting married.

'Who would I marry?' he asked his friends. 'In Holland there are not many women to choose from.'

'Heavens,' his friends said, 'there are women everywhere in Europe and you say there's not much choice!'

'I don't want to marry a European,' Bok said firmly, 'whether she was Dutch, German, French, English, Italian or whatever. She wouldn't be right.'

'Well, aren't there also plenty of Chinese women from Indonesia here? You just have to choose one.'

'I don't know any,' said Bok.

After he said that, his friends took him in turn to their houses or invited him out to restaurants, to shows, picnics and so on, and introduced him to various young women, later followed by introductions to their parents and families. For a few months Bok felt consoled by the new diversions arranged by his friends, even though he had to pay all the expenses of the outings, shows, meals and picnics that they planned. For Bok, money wasn't a consideration at all. The proceeds of his investments were more than enough to pay for everything.

A few months later his friends had run out of candidates for Bok.

'What about it, Bok,' they said, 'we've introduced you to so many girls, isn't there one whom you like? We've even seen you get close to some of them, and then you back off again. What's the matter?'

'I'm sorry,' said Bok, 'choosing a prospective wife is not easy. She has to be your lifelong companion, doesn't she? Certainly many of the girls you brought were pleasant, good looking enough, with charming figures, but they were all money hungry. I got the impression they were all very nice, smiling at me, letting me embrace them and caress their shoulders, I even kissed some of them, because they saw that I was wealthy and had plenty of money.'

'Maybe some of them were after your money, but surely not all of them,' his friends argued. 'Shouldn't you sort them out properly? Mai and Mio were the best. All you have to do is choose between them.'

Bok laughed. 'Who wants to get married, me or you?'

In the end, Bok decided not to choose anyone. He preferred to be free. And as a way out he got a housekeeper to run his household, a Dutchwoman, forty-five years old. Her name was Emma, and she was a widow, with no children.

Bok said to her on the first day, 'I hope you will be happy working for me, and I would like to see you here for a long time, as I don't like changing employees. You will live here and you can have Saturdays and Sundays off. You will look after the whole house and my meals and clothing. And you will also have to work as my nurse because I get asthma attacks from time to time and I need to be helped immediately. Do you understand a little about nursing?'

'I once worked as a nurse,' answered Emma.

'Ah, that's very good. I'll call my doctor later and ask him to show you how to help me with various medications if I get a severe attack. Work well, help me loyally and you won't regret it. You will be well rewarded financially.'

They agreed on the wages which Emma asked for and Bok increased, and he promised extra at the end of the year.

That was ten years ago. Emma worked conscientiously and well, looking after Bok. His asthma didn't get any better because he did not follow one of his doctor's orders. The doctor forbade him to smoke and he obeyed. The doctor also forbade him to drink alcohol but he could not give it up. Emma had accompanied him moving to different places looking for a good climate for him. They had tried living in Nice, Granada in Spain, the southern outskirts of Lisbon in Portugal, Naples, Morocco, Greece, the Adriatic coast in Yugoslavia, but in the end they always came back to Bok's house in The Hague.

When they came back to Holland the last time, Bok said to Emma, 'This is the last time we wander off to those other countries, Emma. Moving around like that only exhausts me. If I must die, let me die here.'

Bok first slept with Emma after she had been working for him for six months. He had an asthma attack at eleven o'clock at night and he pushed the bell to call her. She ran to his bedroom and helped him at once. After his coughing fit subsided Bok asked her to massage his back and chest. He fell asleep as she massaged him. And then when he woke up again he felt sexually aroused, something that had rarely happened for a long time. So the sexual relationship between the two of them began. At first he felt grateful to Emma, and for the first year after she came to help him that night Bok felt a kind of happiness in life come back to him. But then

his asthma recurred more often and his sexual drive dimin-
ished. And then he suddenly realized that he had allowed
himself to become very dependent on Emma. He had to
admit that although they had a sexual relationship, Emma
never showed him or his friends who visited that their
relationship was anything more than that between employer
and employee. Every day her attitude was that of an employee to Bok, keeping the distance between them, not trying
to act even a little affectionately towards him, and showing a
respectful and appropriate attitude to him as her employer.
She did not come if she was not called and never forced her
presence on him. As an employee and household manager
you could say she was exemplary, and this pleased Bok
greatly. Another of her qualities that pleased him was her
patience with him. When his asthma attacked him it often
made him bad-tempered. He got angry easily and exploded.
If he was in that state and Emma was even a little careless or
made a little mistake, or what he thought was a mistake, Bok
would lose his temper and get angry and scold her. But
Emma accepted all this patiently and went on performing
her duties. Bok would immediately apologize to her after he
was calm again. Once he said, 'You are really good, Emma. I
am ashamed of myself for treating you so rudely, but it
comes on with my illness. But I am sorry and want you to
forgive me. Why don't you just leave me if I can't control
myself? You are very patient.'

And Emma said that, as an ex-nurse, she understood sick
people and there was no need for Bok to worry.

Without realizing it, more and more he depended on
Emma for everything. Two years ago he had handed over
the management of his money with his bank to Emma. He
just signed whatever she pushed in front of him. And of
course she knew how wealthy he was.

'You are more than a millionaire, Bok,' Emma said to him
once on her return from the electronics and oil business
which he had bought five years previously and which had

now doubled its price. 'Here is the latest bank statement; your whole fortune, your cash in the bank, your shares in Holland, London and New York, are all worth more than twenty million guilders.'

'But what's the use of all that money to me', said Bok, 'when I can't rid my body of this illness? Maybe I'd get better if I went back to Indonesia.'

Bok was rather startled to see the reaction of Emma, who quickly said in a worried voice, 'And would you leave me behind?'

Bok gave a little laugh, 'Don't be afraid, Emma. Even if I did go I would give you enough money so you wouldn't have to worry about looking for work for years and years. Trust me. I owe you so much.'

Perhaps imagining the possibility that one day Bok would leave Holland, go back to Indonesia and thus leave her too, prompted Emma into making Bok more and more dependent on her. Gradually she urged him to hand over more authority to her, with the excuse of caring for his health and so that he would be free from the various unnecessary little burdens. Bok had given her authority to withdraw money from the bank by signing cheques for ten thousand guilders at a time, and now he no longer needed to sign cheques, money orders and so on to pay his taxes, electricity bills, housekeeping money, doctor's and chemist's bills, house and life insurance and various other things. And Bok felt happy. He was able to listen more to his inner voices reminding him of his former life in Indonesia. And he could meet Reni more often in his memory.

Once he told Emma to try to write a letter to Reni's parents' address and to ask where Reni was now. But Emma persuaded him that there was no point in doing that. That woman would certainly be married, have children and her own life now and would have long forgotten him. Bok gave in but a few days later he felt that he must try anyway to find out what had happened to Reni. 'If Emma won't write the letter, I can write it myself, can't I?' he said to himself. But in the end he did not write it. For too long he had handed everything over to Emma, so he hadn't the will to do it himself.

Bok closed his eyes, feeling rather relieved and he began breathing easily. Emma had gone back to her room. 'Perhaps if I really do want to get better I should return to Indonesia,' he said to himself. But the question came to torment him, 'What would be waiting for you there? Loneliness also, the same as here. Everything which prompted you to leave Indonesia before is still there. Nothing has changed.' And suddenly he regretted that he had lacked the courage to open his heart to Reni.

'It's all too late for me now,' he said to himself. 'I'm more than sixty-five years old. Why don't I marry Emma? Ha,' he laughed at himself. Emma had worked for him for many years and was no longer an attractive looking forty-five-year-old woman. She had got fat, her hair was white, and she had become an ugly, old Western woman. Bok laughed. Emma was really like what he said when he scolded her and threw the Dutch words, 'old witch', at her. Although he would later apologize to Emma for abusing her like that, in his heart he confessed that those words were certainly the right ones to describe her now. Sometimes also, the question arose in his mind as to why Emma was so faithful, going on running his house and nursing him. With his illness and his advancing age, Bok was no longer a good-natured and patient employer. He was more often cranky and feeling bad-tempered and angry. And the question again arose in his mind, 'Why does Emma put up with all this? Because of her high salary? Or does she hope for something else? What?' Finally Bok fell asleep, exhausted by his thoughts.

A week later Bok had another asthma attack. This time it was more terrible than usual. His face went blue. Emma did not know what to do. With things in that state she suddenly went out and came back straight away bringing a sheet of paper and a ball-point pen and told him to sign the paper. Bok took hold of the pen and tried to sign, but before he could do so the attack got worse and the pen slipped from his hand and fell to the floor. His breathing became more laboured, his face was blue, and Emma ran to the phone to call the doctor.

The next day Bok was up out of bed. After the doctor had given him an injection he was able to sleep. Emma was out and she had left a message on the dining-table that she had gone shopping. Bok paced back and forth from room to room. Something was niggling him but he could not explain to himself what it was. When Emma got back and was cooking in the kitchen, Bok came and asked, 'Emma, last night when I had the attack, what paper did you give me to sign?'

Emma looked at him, startled. 'Paper?' she asked. 'I didn't give you any paper to sign.'

'That's strange,' said Bok, troubled again, 'while I was ill I thought I was given a piece of paper to sign. Everything is confused in my memory, perhaps it was a dream. Forget it, don't worry about it,' and he went to the sitting-room. But the restless feeling wouldn't leave him and continued to disturb him. The next day passed and the one after, until Saturday arrived and Emma said she was going off to her friend's place at Leiden and would be back on Sunday afternoon.

'All the medicines are ready near the easy chair, on the small table beside the bed,' she reminded him.

'Thank you, Emma, and I hope you enjoy your weekend.'

After Emma left, he sat watching TV, a soccer match between the Dutch and English teams, which he always followed. But while he was engrossed in watching, he suddenly thought again of his feelings when he was given the paper to sign. Without realizing what he was doing, he went to Emma's room. But when he went to open the door, it was locked. That was surprising. Usually she never locked her door. But he kept duplicate keys of all the rooms. He got the ring of keys and opened the door of Emma's room. He hardly ever went there, except years before when they some-times had sex and he would visit her. He tried to open the drawers of Emma's desk but they were all locked. So was the wardrobe.

'That's strange,' Bok thought, 'what would Emma be wanting to shut away?'

He tried the keys on his key-ring and the drawers opened. He searched them. Ah, only correspondence with her family and her bank book. She had a large deposit in the bank. Then he saw how the amount of the deposit had grown quickly lately. Something hammered at his thoughts. He noticed the dates when her bank deposit increased quickly. He remembered that it was after the time he had given her the authority to sign cheques to withdraw money. 'Hm,' Bok said, 'she's been stealing. Yes, she has.' And then, 'She's served me for a long time. It doesn't matter.' Then he rearranged everything neatly and locked the drawers again. For a moment he hesitated as to whether he would search her wardrobe too. But he remembered the paper that had been pushed at him to sign, and he looked for a key to open it. There were only her clothes. But his hands searched around under the clothes and suddenly his fingers touched some paper and he drew it out.

Bok read it and his expression changed. 'It's criminal. I did not think she was so wicked,' he thought. Because what he read was none other than a will drawn up correctly in official notary's language; and in the will he, Bok, left everything—money in the bank, house, shares—to Emma. She was the sole beneficiary, as a sign of his affection, because she was the only one who had, with loyalty and service, cared for him throughout his life, in sickness and in health, in joy and in sorrow.

'So,' Bok said to himself, 'this must be what Emma has

been after, pretending to serve me, to be loyal and sacrifice herself for me, loving me, going to church every week. She's in league with this notary. He would certainly have asked for a big cut. They are a pair of thieves. Take care! Don't you play around with Bok, even though he is old and sick like this.' Then he laughed to himself. He put the will Emma had drawn up back in the wardrobe and locked it.

Then he telephoned his own notary and asked him to come over.

'Don't you know it's Saturday, Bok?' his friend, the notary, grumbled.

'That's why I am asking you to come,' Bok replied.

He spoke to the notary for a long time, and after he left Bok was still laughing to himself.

After Emma came home on Sunday, Bok did not change his attitude. He was just the same as usual. On the contrary, when they were having breakfast on the Monday, Bok startled Emma by saying, 'Emma, how long have you worked for me?'

'Oh, it's a long time, Bok,' said Emma. 'I'd have to count it up, it's so long. It feels as if I've been with you all my life.'

'Yes, that's what I mean, Emma. It's like we have lived together all our lives, and sometimes I wonder why we don't just get married?'

'Bok, you're joking,' said Emma hopefully.

'No, I often think like that but I always think of my illness and feel it would not be right for me to tie a woman to it. It would be a sin. But I am telling you this, Emma, to show how grateful I am to you. So it's not that I don't notice you.'

For months Bok toyed with Emma like this, like a cat playing with a mouse. And the more he did it the more sadistic were the games he played, one minute giving Emma hope that he would finally marry her, and a few days later destroying that hope. One time he built up her hopes again and even reached the stage of saying, 'Thinking about it again, Emma, it would be fitting for you to inherit all my

wealth later, if we did get married and you became my wife.'
But a week later he changed his mind again. Being teased
like that for weeks by Bok made Emma hope anxiously,
become confused, unsettled, restless, then full of hope with
a pounding heart, and finally it told on her. She lost weight,
her eyes were swollen and tired from loss of sleep, she lost
her appetite and got exhausted easily.

'Eh, Emma,' Bok said to her one morning, 'why have you
suddenly become like this? Your work looking after the
house seems to have deteriorated, your cooking is dreadful,
the kitchen is dirty, and look at you, your clothes are dirty
and not neat as usual, and your hair is messy. I am not
pleased that my housekeeper is slovenly like this. You don't
want me to give you the sack, do you?'

Emma ran out and locked herself in her room, full of
anger towards Bok that she could not let out. But Bok felt
that he had new power. All this time he had felt that Emma
had dominated his life and that he had depended on her
entirely. But now their roles had reversed. Now it was Bok
who had the power and dominated Emma. At times when he
was thinking clearly the question flashed in his mind
whether he was sane to be acting like this. But this question
quickly vanished. In his long, barren life his new game
pleased him very much. Playing the role of a powerful god
who could determine the fate of a human being gave him a
kind of satisfaction he had never felt in his entire life.

But Bok was not able to play his god's role for very long.
One winter's night he had a terrible asthma attack and his
face went blue. Emma did everything she had to, then
shoved a piece of paper at him, which this time he signed.
But his signature was not clear any more, his face was blue,
and Emma did not call the doctor. The next morning she
phoned him after checking and finding that Bok had died in
the night. The doctor diagnosed that Bok had died of a
severe attack of asthma. His friends buried him, and through
a notary Emma demanded Bok's entire fortune. They were

both sure they would get everything.

But another notary, Bok's friend, appeared with a contesting will, and in the examination of the two claims, Emma lost. Because in Bok's will it stressed that he asked the court to declare invalid any will with an illegible signature which he had possibly made when he was having an asthma attack. Irrespective of what date was on such a will, it had been signed when he was not fully aware and clear in his mind; especially if that will stated that he left all or part of his fortune to Emma, his housekeeper. Bok's notary also produced a photocopy of a will, the contents of which were exactly the same as the one Emma produced. According to him a will like this was found in Emma's wardrobe, and once she had tried to push it on to Bok to sign when he was ill. Apparently she did succeed in getting him to sign it when he suffered the attack that took his life.

Emma fainted when she heard the court's decision and did not hear the following paragraphs in Bok's will, which left his entire fortune to the Republic of Indonesia, as soon as Indonesia had succeeded in building a society that knew no racial discrimination and had really implemented *Pancasila* and the 1945 Constitution in a genuine and consistent way.

They say that to this day, Bok's fortune is still waiting in a bank in Holland.

CHAPTER SIX

Whisky

THIS story is from the period of the old order, when President Soekarno still held office as President for Life, Great Leader of the Revolution, Great Fisherman, and all sorts of other greats. This is also a story from the period of Soekarno's guided democracy and guided economy; the period of guided democracy which promised the sovereignty of the people, and the period of guided economy which promised them prosperity but made them suffer and starve. It is a story from the time when Soekarno could sing, 'I come from Blitar, who says the people are hungry?'

This is a story from the time of Haji Jubir Usman (spokesman for the Guided Democracy and Guided Economy Political Manifesto), who unceasingly deceived the Indonesian people. The starving Indonesians in those times could only defend themselves in little ways. And this is the story of a little man who did just that. But unfortunately he did not do it directly to Soekarno or Haji Jubir Usman. He was indeed too small to be able to reach them.

In Jakarta at that time, in the period of the anti-Malaysia confrontation and Soekarno reaching his peak, many foreign journalists arrived. All the international news agencies like Associated Press, United Press, Reuter, Agence France Press, the Russian news agency Tass, not forgetting the Chinese agency Hsinhua, plus the Japanese news bureau Kyodo and various foreign journals like *Time*, *Newsweek* and so on, sent their reporters to Indonesia. Like carrion birds they gathered in Jakarta, waiting for the outbreak of war, with Soekarno ordering his troops to invade Malaysia.

But these foreign reporters often had time on their hands and not enough to do. There was not much that could be reported about Indonesia at that time. The practice in lining up and using weapons by civil servants, old and young, men and women, who were mobilized everywhere, was not interesting enough to be despatched as news. Anyway, who would believe that civil servants, men or women, would really be able to wage war after only a few days' training?

Burt Washington was a journalist for an American bureau and he felt bored in Jakarta. He asked to be replaced and sent to the Vietnam battlefield but his office in New York ordered him to stay on in Jakarta. He was married with two children and had left his family in New York. At a loose end, with not enough to keep him occupied, he began looking around and found a young woman, Ratna, who worked for the Department of Foreign Affairs. He had invited her out to restaurants for dinner a few times and he felt she was becoming ripe for 'picking'. That is what Burt calculated.

His friends saw what he was doing and preparing and they laid bets on his success or otherwise in carrying out his plans. The betting closed at one to ten on. The pay-out would be equal to the bet if Burt succeeded, and ten times the value of the bet if he did not. Only one man was game to bet that Burt would be unsuccessful.

With great interest they followed Burt's preparations. At that time alcoholic drinks were very expensive in Jakarta. One bottle cost tens of dollars and was very difficult to get hold of too. Members of foreign embassies during the years of the old order got rich because they sold their liquor quotas to the black market in Jakarta.

With a lot of trouble and at great expense, thanks to his good relations with some members of the embassy of a country in South-East Asia, Burt managed to buy two bottles of Black & White whisky.

With difficulty he explained to his houseboy to store the two bottles of drink carefully. 'Very expensive ... ex-

pensive ... cost many dollars, uh ... you take good care of it,
yes.'

The houseboy nodded and stored the two bottles of
whisky in the buffet. Then with the houseboy and the cook,
Burt planned his dinner for two with Ratna at his house.
'Don't forget, Saturday night ... you know ... Saturday.'

When Saturday arrived he surprised them, because they
saw him arranging the sitting-room, the dining-room and his
bedroom tidily. He changed the position of the lamps too, to
provide an intimate and romantic atmosphere. On the table
he arranged two candlesticks, purposely choosing long, white
candles. He bought the flowers himself and arranged them
in a vase. He organized the records and chose romantic
songs, and placed them near the electric gramophone.

Afternoon came and Burt bathed, using a special scented
soap he had bought from the shop at the American Embassy,
and splashed a lot of cologne on his body. At five he went to
fetch Ratna. His plan was to take her first to the house of the
British Press Attaché, who was going to screen a film. The
film finished at seven thirty. It was a war film full of love
stories and the ending was very moving. Burt could see how
Ratna was quite impressed by it.

When he invited her to his place for dinner, she nodded
and did not refuse and Burt stepped forward to carry out his
plan. And when in the car he held her hand and she did not
withdraw it, he felt even happier. Near his home he felt
more daring still and caressed her shoulder. And Ratna did
not move away and free her shoulder from his hand. In his
heart Burt was convinced he would achieve his intention that
night. 'So, let them pay up,' he said to himself with satisfaction, thinking of his friends who had bet with him.

Arriving home, he invited Ratna to sit down in the sitting-
room and asked her whether she would like a drink; whisky,
beer or what.

'Ah,' said Ratna, 'I seldom drink alcohol. Just give me
some orange juice.'

'Oh,' Burt said to himself, 'it will be bad luck if she won't drink the whisky.' One of his weapons was the whisky. He hoped that if she drank enough of it, until the alcohol flowed swiftly in her blood, it would be easier for him to trick her. 'What if we change the programme,' he said to Ratna. 'It's almost eight. It would be better if we got on with dinner. Why don't we just have a drink at the table?' Ratna nodded and Burt went out the back to call the cook. He told his houseboy to get the ice ready and get out a bottle of whisky.

Burt put on some Tchaikovsky music, and when the cook came to announce that dinner was ready, he held Ratna's hand and took her to the dining-table. He switched the ceiling lights off. The dining-room was lit by a table lamp in the corner and Burt lit the candles on the table, then sat opposite Ratna.

'Oh, you've made everything so beautiful,' Ratna said.

'Are you happy?' Burt asked. 'You know, this evening is for you. Before we eat, let's have a drink first, shall we?' he invited. He filled two glasses with crushed ice, opened a bottle of whisky and poured it into the glasses.

'Just a little bit for me,' Ratna said.

But Burt ignored her and filled her glass half full, the same as he poured into his own glass.

'Hey, that's too much,' Ratna said, 'I'm not used to drinking whisky.'

'Ah, this isn't much; it's a small glass, isn't it?' said Burt. 'Right, let's drink to our friendship and pray that it will blossom to become a beautiful flower. We have a custom that if we raise our glasses and make a wish, we drink it all down in one swallow. Come on, cheers.'

He raised his glass, threw his head back, and tossed the contents of the glass into his mouth, all at once. But only half of it had gone down his throat when suddenly he tried to stop it. He coughed and coughed and his eyes bulged. His face went red because he was holding his breath, trying to stop the whisky going down his throat, and to bring up what had already passed into his stomach. And suddenly he spat out the whisky that was still in his mouth and coughed violently, his face getting redder. It sprayed all over Ratna's face and body and she, who had just placed the rim of the glass to her lips, leapt up startled, and dropped her glass. It fell on the table, spilling the whisky and wetting the clean white table-cloth. She heard Burt complaining like a strangled buffalo and yelling out for his houseboy, who came running asking, 'What's the matter, sir? What's the matter, sir?'

Burt screamed, 'It's fake whisky! What is this in the bottle? Where's the other bottle?' and the servant ran off to get the other one. Burt opened it quickly, took a small swig and immediately spat it out again on to the houseboy's face. 'It's bad,' he screamed. 'You bloody native, you swapped my whisky with something or other! God-damn you!' The houseboy fled out the back. Burt chased him but soon came back because the servant had run out to the front yard and kept going to the main road.

'Oh, I am sorry, Ratna,' said Burt. 'Please forgive me. I lost control of myself because I am so disappointed that our dinner has been ruined by this rotten houseboy. I'm sure he changed the contents of the bottle with bad tea. Burrrr, the taste of it is still in my mouth. Let us just go to a restaurant. Please clean yourself up in my bathroom.'

Ratna stood up, looked at Burt and in a tight voice said, 'I hate you ... I hate you. I'm going home. You needn't come with me. I am going alone.'

'But why, Ratna, why?'

'You abused your houseboy with very bad words and they hurt me, too ... "bloody native" ... that's what you called him. Well, I'm a native too!'

And she left Burt standing in a daze and slammed the front door as she shut it. Burt stepped up to the table and looked at the two whisky bottles whose contents had been changed and suddenly he pulled the cloth, and the plates, food, glasses, candles and the two bottles were scattered and smashed on the floor.

'Damn, damn!' he cursed.

Afterwards, when it was very late at night and Burt had long been asleep, his houseboy came back quietly, went to his room, collected his clothes and said goodbye to the cook. He felt very pleased to be leaving his job. He had sold the two original bottles of whisky to a whisky wholesaler and had received two fake bottles and several months' wages in payment. Finding work in foreigners' homes was not difficult in Jakarta, especially for an experienced houseboy like him.

CHAPTER SEVEN

Dara

SUDDENLY she appeared in the garden in front of my house; Dara, a young girl of sixteen or seventeen, my daughter's classmate, in second form at Senior High School. I was busy with my orchids. Several pots had been attacked by snails, which had eaten some of the leaves of the dendrobium flowers.

'Good morning, Uncle. Is Yana at home?' And she gave me a sweet smile.

I knew her father and I was surprised at why she had turned up when it was only six thirty in the morning. Her clothing surprised me, too. She was still wearing an evening top ... what are they called ... the clothes that girls and women like wearing when they are going out dancing at night so that they can charm all the men who look at them or dance with them? Dara was wearing that sort of thing, opened low at her breasts, with black satin pants and black high-heeled shoes. Her face was still covered with powder, her lips were red with lipstick, her eyebrows were painted thick and black and her eyelids were coloured blue. Perhaps in a dim dance hall, the way she was dressed and made-up made her look attractive and alluring. But arriving like that early at six thirty in the morning created quite a peculiar impression.

'Eh, Dara,' I said, 'what's the matter? It's only just morning. Did you come straight here from a disco?'

She laughed and only then could it be seen that she was still a young girl. Her make-up made her seem older and like a woman of experience. She reminded me of Nabokov's character Lolita, whereas if she was just dressed normally she was far prettier. I often fail to understand why there are many women, young and old, who don't realize that by dressing and making-up simply their natural beauty shines out more, rather than covering themselves with coats of powder, lipstick, eyebrow paint, false eyelashes, and so on.

I told her to go inside and look for her friend. A quarter of an hour later she and my daughter Yana came out. Dara was wearing their school uniform. 'Of course she borrowed one of Yana's,' I thought. They were the same size and Dara had transformed herself into a high school girl with no lipstick, no powder, no other sorts of paints. Her hair was changed too, tied in a pony tail. Only her eyes looked rather tired from lack of sleep.

'Yana, did you give Dara something to eat?' I asked.

'There's nothing ready yet, Father,' Yana said, 'she's just going to buy something at school. We have to hurry or we'll be late.'

Later when I had breakfast with my wife, I asked her whether she had seen Dara earlier.

'Yes,' my wife said, 'I felt sorry for her.'

'Why sorry? She's a very naughty girl. It's certain she was out all night last night at a party and, not daring to go home to her parents' place, came straight here and on to school. We know her parents, don't we? If they investigated whether she spent the night here, it would be difficult for us, wouldn't it? If we said "yes" we'd be lying, but if we said "no" they'd be very angry with Dara. Perhaps it would be better if I phoned her father or mother now and told them what happened. Who knows if they have been running around frantically looking for her all night.'

'Hush,' my wife said, 'don't be in such a hurry. It's not certain yet, is it? Who knows if Dara will tell her parents the truth. We don't know what happened last night, do we? Also, it's none of our business.'

'Yes, but what if goings on like that have a bad influence on your daughter?'

'Ah,' my wife said, 'your daughter is sixteen years old. Do you think young girls like that don't know anything and are ignorant about the relationships of boys and girls? Can't they read and hear stories from their older friends? Neither their parents nor teachers can always supervise their behaviour every minute.'

That night I got the story from my wife, who had got it from Yana, who had in turn got it from Dara, that first of all, the previous night Dara had gone with her parents to her uncle's birthday party. From there she went dancing with her mother and father to a disco at an international hotel. There she met her friends and their dancing party grew.

They were having a good time when her mother and father began to quarrel. Indeed, during the past few years they often fought, Dara told Yana. Moreover, if he had a fight with his wife, her father used to leave the house and just spend the night at a large hotel. He would stay there for days and not come home. But the previous evening her parents had quarrelled for the first time in public, and the fuss was over a stupid matter. Her father, who had been drinking, saw a foreign woman, a disco singer, sitting at a table and invited her to dance. Her mother was not pleased; firstly because her father left their table, and secondly because he and the singer were holding each other very closely. Finally, her father went home by himself and her mother went home by herself, and Dara, because she was upset, went on dancing with her friends till one o'clock in the morning. Feeling she did not want to see her parents, she booked a room at the hotel. The hotel man, who knew her parents, gave her a room. She had woken early and remembered she had to face an exam the next day at school and turned up early as she did at our place.

'The moral is, don't leap to conclusions,' my wife said, ending the story.

For a long time after that Dara never came to our house. When our daughter Yana graduated from high school, as a present we gave her a holiday in Medan to visit her grand-mother and other relatives there. She went with her cousin, who was also a girl of her own age.

'Instead of flying,' they said, 'we'd rather go by boat. You could give us the difference between the plane tickets and the boat tickets as extra spending money.'

'Very clever,' I grumbled, but of course they won in the end.

When we took them down to the Jakarta Lloyd boat at Tanjung Priok and arrived at their cabin, suddenly there was a voice at the door shouting excitedly, 'Yana, Uncle, Aunty!'

'Dara!' Yana shouted, standing up and hugging the young woman who stood at the door wearing a stewardess's uni-form. If Yana hadn't shouted 'Dara!', I would not have recognized her any more, even though it was only about two years since I'd seen her.

She came and greeted us and I said to her, 'Do you work on this boat? How long have you been here?'

'Only six months, Uncle.'

'I almost didn't recognize you,' I said to her, 'you've grown into a young woman.'

And indeed there were great changes in her. From the face and appearance of a fresh young high school girl the morning she came to my orchid garden, there now stood in front of me a young adult woman. Her body had filled out, the awkwardness and shyness of a young girl facing her elders had vanished entirely. Her make-up was now appro-priate and not overdone, enough to show off the attractive characteristics of her face and body. She looked really pretty and appealing.

'Right,' I said when the ship's whistle told visitors to go ashore, 'I'll entrust these two girls to you, all right Dara?'

'Everything is fine, Uncle; don't worry,' she answered gaily.

Later, when Yana returned home, I got another story about Dara from my wife. Yana told my wife that Dara was not 'fine' now. Apparently they too had not seen each other for a long time until they met again on the ship. Dara left school when she was not promoted a class and since then she no longer associated with her school friends. She told Yana that a big breakup had occurred between her mother and father. Although they were not divorced, her father in practice did not live at their house any more. He had bought his own house and lived there. 'I hate my father,' she told Yana. 'All the time he keeps changing the women who live there with him. Some only stay for a month, some make it to two or three, and there are foreign women. I also don't understand why Mother puts up with his behaviour. Is it because he continues to give her plenty of money to keep house? Shouldn't she as a woman and a human being have the courage to defend her honour? She just lets herself be trodden on by Father. I don't understand her, especially as she plays around with other men too, to get even.'

Once in a while Dara visited her father, but only to ask for money. And her father always gave it to her, however much she asked for. 'My father must be involved in corruption,' Dara told Yana. 'How could he have so much money, even if he was a bank director? We are ruined ... Father is ruined, and Mother, and I am too, Yana.' It was as though she felt the need to let out all her feelings to someone. On the ship, for several days of the sea trip, she had met Yana, to whom she could pour out everything in her heart. And her story was actually very moving although, according to Yana, Dara told it interspersed with laughing too. 'But because of that I felt more moved,' Yana told her mother. Dara also told Yana that she'd had various boy-friends and described her sexual experiences to Yana and her cousin in detail too.

'Good heavens,' I said, 'we sent these two young girls by boat to Medan, but it seems they got sex lessons on board.'

After that I didn't hear anything else about Dara for a

long time. And from that time on I took more careful note of Yana's behaviour, frightened in case she was infected with Dara's disease as a result of the sex lessons she had received from her on the boat. But I saw she was the same as usual. She still brought home her new boy-friends whom she changed once or twice a month.

Six months later I saw Dara again at the bowling-alley. A large group of our family went there to have a competition. My children challenged me to a match. They knew I hardly ever played ... very rarely. But I had once played in Baguio and once in Seattle and I knew I could bowl the ball straight to the target. We played and I lost and the children were very excited because the bet was that if I lost I would treat them to a meal in a restaurant. When Dara arrived a foreign man had his arm around her shoulder. She quickly greeted us and introduced her friend, an Italian.

I saw Dara immediately draw Yana aside and saw them both very busy talking. To fill in the time waiting for them to exchange their personal information I talked too, to the Italian. I asked whether he'd been long in Indonesia, what his job was here, had he known Dara long, and so on. He said that he sold Italian industrial goods made by the factory where he worked. He would be in Indonesia for about three months and Dara was working with him as his temporary secretary.

Then Dara apparently finished giving her news to Yana and we said goodnight to them. On the way out I commented to my wife, 'His secretary ... secretary in bed most likely. Foreigners are crude, they just play around with Indonesian women because they have the money to do it.'

For a long time I have been annoyed and upset seeing the behaviour of foreign men in our country since it was opened up to foreign capital investment. When I see foreigners embracing young Indonesian women in discotheques, restaurants, coffee shops, international hotels, in cinemas, I am always upset. Because clearly they are only using these

women as a target for their sex needs and are buying them. I
say to everyone, 'If I were your age I would thrash men who
dared to have affairs with Indonesian women without being
married. But at my age, if I had a fight in public, it would be
ridiculous.' But so far I see my agitation has had no effect.
On the contrary, more and more frequently I see foreigners
using Indonesian women, especially Japanese tourists. Yes, I
know too that many Indonesian women are married by the
foreign men and taken back to their countries, but as far as I
can see only a few of them have happy marriages. A large
number of them separate after two or three years of marriage.
In France also there are women from the Jatiluhur district,
who were married and taken home by former French
workers who had built the Jatiluhur dam. Many of them are
divorced. When I was in Paris once, I heard that a lot of
them turned up in Spain to work as domestic servants
because they were left to their own fate after being divorced.
Many also asked for help from the Indonesian Embassy to
be sent home to Indonesia. But it wasn't an easy problem
because they had become French citizens and held French
passports.

When we were eating at the restaurant Yana reported
what Dara had told her. 'Mother,' she said, 'Dara said that
she wanted to kill her father. She said she was disgusted
with his behaviour, which was more and more crude and
very insulting to her mother. But she can no longer respect
her mother either because she has such a weak attitude. Her
father thinks that if he keeps giving Dara money, he can buy
her affection.'

'That was her new Italian boy-friend, wasn't it?' I asked.

'Yes,' said Yana, 'Dara said they met at a discotheque.'

'What did I tell you,' I said to my wife.

'Yes, but she said she also works with Italians,' Yana
added.

'I am amazed', I said, 'at why Indonesian women are so
attracted to foreigners. Maybe they think foreign men have a

lot of money, and if they are taken to America, Australia, England, Germany or France they'll be certain to live happily there and have everything they want. They don't know that society in those industrialized countries has other problems that are even more dangerous. They don't know they will suffer from loneliness there. They'll have to work harder and look after their houses themselves too. If they have no money there, they're finished, and more important still, they don't understand that foreign men are not ... circumcised.... How could they stand it?'

'Hush,' my wife said.

'You are porno, Father,' one child yelled.

'You're a rude old man, Father,' said Yana.

More than a year later I heard another story about Dara from Yana. I was not in Indonesia when it happened. I was on an assignment abroad. In the end Dara's father's corruption was exposed and he was arrested. Dara asked Yana to go with her one day to see him. Dara arrived at the jail strikingly dressed and made-up. Anyone who saw her would conclude that she was a woman of experience, open to offers. Her father, when he saw her, got that impression too. Apparently a few months in jail had aroused some awareness in him. He gave Dara advice, all the while mentioning God's name, and told her to wake up and to go back to school, become a good, virtuous woman, ask God's pardon, and all sorts of other things. And the longer her father talked like that, the more Dara's expression changed and the more she altered the way she was sitting, crossing her legs more provocatively so that her thighs were exposed high up. The more she sank back low on the seat, the louder her father spoke until finally he shouted, 'Dara, sit up properly and listen to your father!'

Dara leapt to her feet, pointed at her father and said full of anger and hate, 'Oh Father, why is it that you are only giving me this fine advice now? Why didn't you give it before, with your own behaviour as an example, when you and Mother were living together? You have destroyed our happiness, Mother is destroyed and I am destroyed. Why are you angry with me now? I am only following in your footsteps. You think you can wipe out your sins to Mother with money. You don't know that I haven't had a father or a mother for a long time.'

And suddenly Dara burst into tears, pulled Yana's hand and ran out of the visitor's room at the jail. Yana still managed to turn and look at Dara's father. He covered his face with his hands and wept.

For a long time I was deep in thought when I heard Yana's story. Feelings of compassion slipped into my heart. I saw my wife's eyes glistening and my sons could not speak, and I asked, 'And what about the Italian?'

'Oh, that wasn't serious, Father. He had to go home before the three months were up because he didn't succeed in selling his goods.'

'Ah, he didn't know the way. Usually Italians are good at opening doors by paying bribes. In their country corruption is a matter of course like it is here. What is Dara's job now?'

'She's not working any more. But she has no financial problems. She can just go to her mother's or her father's place. Although he's been caught, he is still rich.'

Later, Dara's father was brought to trial. For weeks the newspapers were full of the story. He was sentenced to two years' jail and fined several million rupiahs. I don't remember the amount, but rumour had it that he was still wealthy because he was clever at putting away his money. 'The judge was bribed too,' a friend commented.

Not long after her father was sentenced, one day when I came home from the office I saw Yana and Dara busy chatting while they listened to the music of the young nowadays. Dara stood up and greeted me. I was amazed to see her; she was completely changed. She was wearing simple clothes and no make-up. She wasn't wearing any lipstick at all, the blue eyeshadow was missing, her eyebrows were not drawn, the false eyelashes were gone, and she looked serene. Her face glowed and the light in her eyes was fresher.

'Uncle, I would like to stay at your home for a few days. May I, Uncle? I want to taste normal family life.' And she looked at me hopefully.

I gave her a hug. 'Of course you can. We are pleased you came. Does Mother know?' I asked Yana.

'Mother is pleased, too,' Yana replied.

As usual, I was the last one to get the report. Dara stayed with us for a week, then went back to her mother's house. Yana as usual reported to her mother first, and only later did I hear the story from my wife.

'I'm happy to see the change in Dara,' I said to my wife, 'I pray she's really found herself again, the poor child. How could she change to become good again so suddenly?'

'According to what she told Yana, it's her father who has changed, and really come to his senses,' my wife related. 'You remember Dara was angry with her father when she visited him in jail? Apparently he was very shaken by his daughter's words. Somehow or other he was apparently able to convince Dara that he had woken up and was determined to mend his ways. He has even healed his relationship with his wife. He asked his wife and daughter to forgive and pardon him, and in his letter to them he begged them to help him improve himself to become a good husband and father. He confessed to being lost all this time and reminded them that God pardons every sinner who comes to his senses and begs His forgiveness.'

'Thank heavens for that,' I said. 'You know it is very rare that from the collapse of a life like that, the pieces and ruins can be gathered and reorganized to become a new life. That is really a gift from God. I'm sure God forgives him because He sees that his being lost was not one hundred per cent his fault.'

'Oh you men, you always try to defend each other,' my wife said indignantly.

'It's not a matter of defending a fellow man,' I said, 'Dara's father is also a victim of the state of our society now, isn't he? Everyone is corrupt, moral values are destroyed, money and wealth have become the measure of happiness. Aren't you lucky I don't have much money and don't have the chance for corruption...?'

CHAPTER EIGHT

The Healer

AFTER faithfully carrying us on safari from West Java, through Central and East Java, across to the islands of Bali and Lombok and back again to Bali, then to Banyuwangi, when it entered the town of Probolinggo in the late afternoon, my pick-up truck started to give trouble. Getting in and out of first gear was easy, but from first gear to second and third was very difficult. And if I was in second or third gear and wanted to shift to first or back it was also very difficult. Since arriving at the outskirts of Probolinggo I had just let the pick-up use first gear and slowly entered town looking for a hotel, because it was nearly sunset. In the middle of town I went into a hotel that was small but looked clean.

Fortunately there was a room. I asked the manager to find me a mechanic. That evening while I was sitting on the veranda I saw a Mercedes Tiger come into the grounds of the hotel and stop in front of the veranda. A woman of Chinese descent got out, followed by her female servant carrying a young girl, and a Chinese man. They passed the veranda and headed for their room. The hotel manager, a middle-aged man, said, 'That poor mother and father, they've been here three days and still haven't been able to get treatment for their daughter.'

'What's wrong with her?' I asked.

'She's paralysed, sir. She caught polio when she was small.'

'Why, in three days, haven't they been able to see a doctor?' I asked in surprise.

'Oh, you don't know, do you, that for the past three months Probolinggo has been in an uproar because of a healer. His name is Pak Gede. He opens his practice in the town square after evening prayers. Look, sir, not just people from in and around Probolinggo come to him for treatment, but from other districts; from Surakarta, Malang, Madura, Yogya, Semarang, and that family just now comes from Bandung. See their car, with the D number plates?'

I stood up a moment and looked in the yard. It was indeed true. The Mercedes Tiger had D number plates. Shortly afterwards the woman servant came out and I said, 'Did you manage to see the healer just now?'

'Oh, not yet, sir. Poor mistress and master, sir, they always miss out. For three days now it's been over too quickly. Yesterday they waited till twelve o'clock for him but their turn was still a long way off and the healer wanted to go home.'

The servant then excused herself. She had to get food from a restaurant near the hotel. This reminded me that my stomach was hungry too and had to be given dinner. I went to the restaurant to eat, and after that I went to watch the mechanic who was working on my pick-up.

Then I went to my room and slept. The next morning after breakfast I sat around again on the veranda waiting for the mechanic. The hotel watchman told me that the day before he had worked till one o'clock in the morning and the car wasn't finished yet. The mechanic had left me a message to wait for him to come because something had to be welded.

Not long after, the Chinese couple came out of the restaurant and sat at the table beside me.

'Excuse me,' I said addressing them, 'I hear that you brought your child here to be treated by Pak Gede. Were you able to see him last night?'

'Ah, not yet, sir,' the husband answered. 'Yesterday we waited again till midnight but still couldn't see him. His assistant said that hopefully we will tonight.'

'Has your daughter been ill for long?'

'Sadly, since she was small, sir; since she was four years old when she got polio,' answered the wife. 'We only brought her home from Germany a month ago.'

And she described their travels taking their beloved daughter to all the doctors that they heard had the knowledge to heal her. A friend had mentioned the name and address of a doctor in Germany, whom it was said could reactivate muscles and frozen nerve channels. They were in Germany for two months trying treatment with him but it was unsuccessful and finally he raised his hands, unable to do anything else.

'It cost us a great deal,' the wife said. 'Before that we had taken our child to America, to Boston. That was unsuccessful, too. We were only there two weeks and the doctors who examined her said nothing else could be done for her. We were not satisfied, and being in America we checked this out with several doctors. We have been to France, to Holland and to England. We have taken her to Lourdes. When we got home from Germany we heard from someone in Bandung about this Pak Gede. We decided to come immediately. For our child's sake, what's the good of hanging on to our money? Who knows, everything is in the hands of God, isn't it? Who knows if God, who is all powerful, wants our child to be cured in Probolinggo,' she said full of hope.

Then they told me that they owned a large textile factory in Bandung and of their travels to find someone who could cure their child. 'For these past ten years, two or three times a year, we have taken her abroad chasing doctors that our friends tell us about. You know, sir, if we did not take her we'd regret it later. Why not try?'

'Have you tried all the healers in our country?' I asked. 'They say there is also a healer with mystical power in Blitar.'

'We have,' the wife answered. 'I was there for a month but there was no success.'

'What about the ones in Cimacan near Cipanas, and around Pasar Minggu in Jakarta?'

'Oh, we've been to all of them. We've tried all the well-known healers in Indonesia, even as far away as Sumatra, Kalimantan and Ambon.'

It seemed as if there was pride in her voice, telling how she loved her child, didn't care about the cost or succumb to exhaustion. She was prepared to take her child anywhere at all and would pay anything at all to find a cure for her.

Her husband was silent, nodding in agreement with his wife's words.

While we were chatting thus, the hotel manager arrived.

'Good morning, sir; good morning, madam,' he said. 'Were you able to see Pak Gede last night?'

'No,' the wife replied.

'Be patient, madam. You must endure the wait. Just look at the long line of people who have registered. But Pak Gede is demonstrating his mystical powers. Once I went to see him myself, two weeks ago. A child who could not walk, like yours but younger, about eight years old, was carried by her father to the place where Pak Gede was. All the people—there were probably hundreds of them that night—were gathered in the village square to watch him treating people. The child was placed in front of him. He concentrated for a while, then filled a glass with water from a pitcher and put some frangipani flowers in it. He held the child's feet, then brushed them with water from the glass.

'Then he said loudly and firmly to the child, "Stand up!" Believe it or not, sir, with my own eyes I saw the child who was paralysed just before, slowly and with a great deal of difficulty, stand up, and when her father went to try and help her he was forbidden to by Pak Gede, and finally she stood all by herself. The crowd present held their breath in great wonder and you could clearly hear many voices saying, "Yes, Allah". After the child stood up Pak Gede again wiped her feet with water from the glass, concentrated a moment, opened his eyes and said to the child in a clear voice,

"Walk!" And the child walked, sir, not stepping smoothly as healthy people like us do, still stiffly, but walking.'

We fell silent hearing his story. The mother's eyes shone with hope. Only the father's expression did not change. I never believed in happenings like that caused by the magical powers of healers. In my heart I was suspicious in case it was set up on purpose to demonstrate the healer's powers, whereas the child was not really paralysed, and could walk, but was told by the healer to pretend she could not. Who could guarantee that it was not play acting, the sly cunning of the healer arranged beforehand with the father and child? Who could guarantee that the man was really the child's father? But seeing the hopeful expression in the mother's face, I didn't have the heart to express my disbelief. I was more suspicious as to why they had not been able to reach the healer in more than three days. Possibly he was frightened he would not be able to cure the child with polio, and thus would lose the crowd's faith and, of course, his income.

'How much did he ask for the cure?' I asked the manager.

'They say he didn't ask for anything, it's just up to those who want to give,' he answered.

This too was the tactic of all healers. They did not ask for payment, because indeed they were instructed not to by the source that gave them the magical power. If they asked for payment, the power would disappear. But of course the person who was treated, especially if once in a while he happened to recover, would pay as much as he could. It's not surprising that many famous healers live very well, own big houses, land and fields. I have never heard of a well-known healer, visited by many people asking for treatment, who lived in poverty, even though he never asked for payment.

I introduced myself to them, because I thought I really did not know them formally, even though we had been talking together so much. I gave my card to the husband and he gave his to me.

Then the mechanic arrived and said that he had to weld a few parts. I gave him some money.

'I pray that your child will be successfully cured by the Probolinggo healer,' I said to them. 'I'd really like to know what happens. If I ever come to Bandung, may I call in to find out?'

'Oh please do. We will be pleased to receive you,' the father said.

I left them and joined a small party leaving the hotel to visit the peak of Mt. Bromo.

When I got back at 8 p.m., I saw that the Mercedes Tiger with the D number plates was not in the yard. Apparently they had already gone to Pak Gede. Not long after, the mechanic came to say he had fixed my car. I took him around to try the gears. They weren't yet smooth as usual, but adequate, and could get in and out of first and shift to second and third and back again. I paid him the amount decided on earlier and added a tip. He went off happily.

The next day, after having breakfast, paying my hotel bill and preparing to leave for Surabaya, I saw the couple from Bandung come on to the veranda heading for the restaurant. I approached them and reached out my hand to say goodbye.

'Are you leaving now?' the father asked.

'Yes,' I said, 'I'm two days late already with my car trouble. I'm off to Surabaya this morning. How was last night?'

'We got there, we got to Pak Gede. He examined her and we were told to come back in two days' time because he said the child had been paralysed for too long and he needed time to treat her.'

'I pray she gets better. Goodbye.' We shook hands and I left.

For months I thought nothing more of this meeting in Probolinggo or of the healer Pak Gede and his magical powers that drew hundreds of people every night to the square in the middle of Probolinggo. One day when I happened to be in Bandung, I opened my wallet where I kept my car papers and licence and suddenly a card fell out—Agus Prawirakusuman, director, Pangrango textile factory. There were the home and office addresses and telephone numbers. It was him, the father who had taken his paralysed child to Probolinggo, and I felt a great desire to know what had happened. It was 10 a.m. and of course he would already be at the office. I phoned him there and was put through immediately. I explained to him who I was and that we had once met in Probolinggo.

'Oh yes, I remember you, you are a journalist, aren't you? Please come on over, you can have a look at my factory at the same time.'

When I arrived at the factory, the watchman had been told of my coming. The secretary was waiting in the front room and I was taken straight in. When Agus saw me come in he stood up at once to greet me, and his guest, who was sitting with his back to the door, turned around.

'Good heavens, it's my friend, Mang Didi! I had no idea we were going to meet here,' I shouted at him.

Didi was my friend from the time of the 1945 revolution. He was a retired general from the Silawangi division. He jumped up from his chair and embraced me. We hadn't seen each other for a long time.

'I heard from Agus that you were coming, so I waited. We haven't had a good talk for ages.'

'Well, this is a happy day for me,' Agus said, 'being able to bring two old friends together. Didi and I are like brothers,' he said explaining to me. 'If he hadn't helped me I'd probably have died when Bandung was attacked by the Dutch forces. He helped me, my parents and three other brothers to make a quick escape. What about having lunch together,' he invited, 'but before you have a look around the factory, have a drink first. What would you like, coffee, tea, chocolate or beer?'

'Tea and no sugar,' I said.

After the tea came I asked how his child was. He shook his head.

'How can my child be well again? I've accepted the facts for a long time but my wife still wants to keep on trying.'

Then he invited us to look around his factory. It was quite interesting because in a new part of it he had installed modern weaving machines.

'Actually, these machines can be supplemented with a kind of robot which can connect broken threads. But I don't want to use a robot because this would mean less workers would be needed. Didi always advises me not to forget to open up as many jobs as possible, don't you, Didi?'

Didi nodded. 'This Agus is a cold-blooded capitalist,' Didi laughed, teasing him. But he added, 'Actually, Agus has become a real Indonesian. In the time of the revolution, his father also helped my troops a great deal with clothing and medical supplies.'

After we had a look at the factory, Agus invited us to eat. He took us to a restaurant with delicious Sundanese cooking and after we had eaten he invited us to his home. He said his wife would be very pleased to see me and Didi.

'I'm sorry,' I said, 'I have an appointment at three at I.T.B.'

'And I have to go home, too,' said Didi, 'there's a guest coming.'

'Another time,' we promised.

We parted. I took Didi home and he said that if I wasn't doing anything that night to drop in at his place, or better still, come for dinner.

'But Neng (the name of his wife—all his friends called her 'Neng') doesn't know you are inviting me for dinner tonight.'

'Ah, that's all right. I'll tell her later. She will be happy to cook for you. I'm not just saying this, but she always says you are the friend of mine that she likes most. Sometimes she makes me jealous.' Didi had a good laugh at his own joke.

That evening Neng served me vegetable soup with tamarind which she knew I was very fond of, spicy sauce, vegetables and fish. They had six children from eight to twenty-two years of age. It was a very happy, noisy meal that night. The father, children and mother all liked having fun, and around the dining-table it was noisy with laughing and shouting.

'This is a big Malay family, but it's like this....' Didi grumbled although he looked very happy, 'I'm a general, am I not, but which of these rascals will obey me?'

'Come on, Father,' his smallest child, a girl, said. 'Don't believe him, Uncle. If Father gets angry we all run and hide and warn everyone. We say "Look out, there's a hurricane, a hurricane!"' The children all laughed.

'Well just look at that, they are laughing at me. We old ones wouldn't have dared to joke with our parents like that, that's true, isn't it?'

'Look,' I said to them, 'if we were invited to eat like this with our father, we would feel very reluctant and uncomfortable. We were not allowed to be noisy like you, but just had to be quiet.'

'Fathers were ferocious in the olden days,' the youngest cut in.

'That's right,' Didi said, 'you don't realize you are lucky having a father like me. You hit the jackpot, don't you know?'

'Oh, did we?' they shouted noisily.

But I saw that his children knew enough discipline. After the meal they asked to be excused to do their study.

'It's lovely having a big family, isn't it, Di?' I said.

'It's all Neng's fault. She didn't want family planning from the very beginning.'

'Oh, just have a nice gossip. Give away our secrets, won't you,' his wife said, teasing him.

We laughed. I was happy in the embrace of such affectionate family life. We chatted about this and that and the conversation turned again to Agus Prawirakusuman. I told of my meeting with them in Probolinggo and of how moved I was to see the hope shining in his wife's face when she heard the hotel manager's story about the healer's magical powers.

'Tell him, dear, the even sadder story,' said Didi to his wife.

'You tell him. I have to go out the back and see Bibi. She said earlier she had a headache and stomach pains. I hope she's not getting gastro.'

Neng left us and I urged Didi to tell the story.

'I know the story from the beginning. When their child got polio, Susan, that's the wife, was on a tour to Australia with her friends. She is from a wealthy family, and indeed her hobby was visiting foreign countries. But she didn't travel just for the sake of travel. Her Chinese blood, expert in business, is still strong within her. While she toured she always noted the new clothing designs and photographed them and studied the fashions, and thereby was able to help her husband's work.

'He telephoned her and said that their child was ill, but at that stage the doctor could not say what the illness actually was. And when Susan did come home, it was only then that she knew it was polio. She could not forgive herself that she had not come home straight away after receiving the news from her husband. She felt guilty because she had not paid enough attention and that was why her child was incurably ill. For a long time she has actually not been quite normal. She's not really crazy, but she's suffering from shock and feels that she has sinned against her child. In the first years, I believe, she was really impelled by her great desire to find a doctor or anyone at all who could treat her daughter. Fortunately they are wealthy people. Just imagine the cost of it, two or three times a year going abroad to chase doctors everywhere....

'But after a few years of doing this sort of thing, her child was always incurable, and she was told this by every well-known doctor in every country they visited. Any sane person should have accepted the fact, however bitter it was. Agus has long accepted it and resigned himself to his child's condition. The child is really to be pitied. I've said to Agus and Susan, "Wouldn't it be better if the child was put into a clinic which could train her to walk with the aid of equipment invented especially for children who have had polio?" But because Susan was taking the child everywhere she didn't get the chance to be taught to help herself. She has to be carried everywhere by a servant, even if it is only two steps, and she hasn't learnt anything at all. Just imagine, to this day, that child can hardly read. It's really terribly sad. Yet she's a sweet child and if you speak to her, her thoughts are really clear. But her mother.... I once said to Agus that the person who was more in need of treatment was Susan herself.'

'And what does Agus think?'

'He told me he's known that for a long time.'

'But didn't he do anything, like, for example, take Susan to a specialist? Who knows, a psychiatrist might be able to help her.'

'Agus tried once, but Susan wouldn't go. She said she wasn't mad and, what's more, she was angry with Agus.'

Just then Neng returned from out the back.

'I think Bibi has a cold,' she said.

'I've told him about Susan. People who don't know would think how happy Agus and Susan are; wealthy, owning a large textile factory, traipsing abroad all the time. But their life is full of a heavy burden of sorrow. Isn't it better to be a poor, retired general, with no textile factory, but happy with his family, Neng?' Didi said to his wife.

Neng just smiled, looking lovingly at her husband.

CHAPTER NINE

Life is a Game of Roulette

MAHDI was used to taking risks with his life. When he was eighteen years old, at the time of the war of independence against the Dutch, he had joined in the fighting. Who knows where he got the saying from, but if their forces were bottling the enemy up or attacking their position, Mahdi was always one of the daredevils and before the battle began he would always say, 'Life is a game of roulette; if you are not bold, you will not win'—and then it was as though he had no fear of death at all. And during the war of independence, his luck playing roulette with enemy bullets was certainly good. Mahdi always won. He was never even wounded. His unfailing enthusiasm made him respected by his comrades and liked by his superiors. When the war was over, Mahdi had reached the rank of first lieutenant, so quickly had he gained promotion.

But he also resigned immediately from the army. His commander tried to persuade him not to go. 'Soon there will be opportunities for young officers like you to get education, and a good career is open to you in the army. Why do you want to resign? The army needs officers with great spirit and intelligence like you.'

And Mahdi replied that he had joined the army before because he felt it his duty as a loyal young man, but that being in the army, even if he later became a general, was not the aim of his life.

'Then what do you want to be?' asked his commander, who really looked after his men.

'It's not that I consider life as a soldier lacking in prestige, sir,' he replied, 'no, but if we are in the army we are not free, are we? We are bound by discipline. Our lives are controlled by authority. Our time is not our own. I want to be free, sir, to be a member of a free society, to be my own master, a free human being shaping himself, not ordered around by other people, but with full responsibility for his own actions, good and bad. Isn't this life only a game of roulette, sir? Where we place the bet is our decision. If the ball stops on the number that we choose, we win, if not, we lose, and it's all our full responsibility.'

'Don't forget,' his commander said, 'there are laws and regulations which govern our behaviour as citizens, and spiritual values that govern our behaviour as human beings.'

'Oh I don't have any difficulties with all that, sir,' Mahdi replied.

His commander took a long, deep breath. He was really sad to see Mahdi determined to resign from the army.

'Well,' he said, 'I pray that you will succeed in civilian life, and I will hand on your request to my superiors.'

Mahdi got out of the army when he was just twenty-five years old. He had great business talent, and saw many gaps he could fill. In the first five years in his own business he succeeded in going into partnership with a Chinese merchant. Mahdi proved to his friend, Siau Bun Ho, that a lot of profit could be drawn from a shipping business with small boats connecting various places on the North Sumatra coast along the Straits of Malacca and across to places on the coast of Malaysia and Singapore. They began with two boats carrying agricultural products and different kinds of commodities from Sumatra and Aceh between various places on both sides of the Straits of Malacca.

Their shipping business prospered, thanks to Mahdi working very hard, studying his own field, accompanying their ships, and fostering good relations with their customers.

In 1960 he suggested to Siau Bun Ho that they expand the business to become a national shipping network. He left for Jakarta and had a stroke of good luck. He met his ex-commander who had a high position in the Defence Department and who gave him a recommendation to officials of the Ministry for Communications.

Shortly after, Mahdi obtained permission to open an inter-island shipping enterprise and, with Siau Bun Ho, he established their shipping company called the Lake Toba Line. They started off with two medium-sized ships and these they called the *Lake Toba I* and *Lake Toba II*.

'And we'll call all our ships *Lake Toba III*, *IV*, *V* and so on,' Mahdi said to Siau Bun Ho.

Siau Bun Ho was happy being in partnership with Mahdi because Mahdi was very open and handed over to him administration problems, financial arrangements, and internal organization. Mahdi felt happier working on outside connections, chasing customers and new enterprises, and developing new ideas. Every time he put forward a new idea which would increase business and thus bring a profit, if Siau Bun Ho, whose nature was always to have a careful attitude, said, 'Think about it first, we must be careful,' then Mahdi would say, 'Life is a game of roulette, Bun Ho, this will be sure to land on our number.' And he would coax and convince Siau Bun Ho on and on until finally Siau accepted his idea. Mahdi's calculations were never wrong. Moreover, after their shipping company was developing well and its name was well known in world business circles, then, if they needed finance for new projects Mahdi was developing, the banks were very happy to give them credit. With bank credit behind them their business grew quickly.

Mahdi in those years was really like a true roulette player with a very bright star. He was like a person with magical powers; anything he touched turned to gold. And he showed too that he never forgot his former army friends. He and Siau Bun Ho had moved to Jakarta because their business was now centred there. But he always tried to find his former comrades first if there was a new job vacancy.

Mahdi had achieved success and results with bets in his life of roulette.

'And now, Di,' his friend Siau Bun Ho said to him, 'there's another roulette gamble that you'll have to take one day.'

'What do you mean?' Mahdi said.

'How old are you now? Try and count,' said Siau Bun Ho.

'I'm thirty-eight. Why?'

'Oh my friend, that's more than old enough. You are wealthy, you've got enough money, why do you still live alone?'

Mahdi was confused a moment, then laughed and was quickly silent again. Then, 'Yes, by God!' he said, 'You are right. Hey, Bun Ho, do you know, all this time I've really been oblivious to the fact that there are women in this world. I've just been so absorbed in our work.'

He stopped and looked at his friend and frowned, his sharp eyes on Siau Bun Ho.

'Eh, what's the matter? Why are you looking at me like that?' asked Siau Bun Ho.

'I should be angry with you, friend,' said Mahdi. 'You are cunning. Why is it that only now you remind me that there are women in this world who can attract a man's heart? You let me work hard for years, while you got married and had a nice time making children. Come on, confess, you villain!'

'Ah, so you've just rejoined the human race, Di,' his friend said, laughing. 'You'd better look seriously for a wife. Or aren't you any good at finding one yourself. Do you want me to find one for you?'

Mahdi was silent a moment. Then, 'It's not your business, is it? But Siau, they say, why, if you want to eat meat, do you buy a whole cow? Isn't it easier to buy a piece?'

'Listen, a wife is not a cow, make no mistake about that!'

But after their discussion, Mahdi did a lot of thinking and

he looked at the young women he knew with new eyes. He was quite fond of one of them, Aidah. He knew her parents and sometimes visited her home. But all this time he just considered her as a friend. However, now, with marriage on his mind, he felt more and more attracted to her. She seemed to be calm and patient and those were the qualities he needed in a wife.

For a long time he felt uncertain and when he told Siau Bun Ho how he felt, his friend said, 'How come you yourself, who always say life is a game of roulette, have now become uncertain? Aidah is right for you!'

Mahdi finally decided to marry Aidah. His roulette gamble with marriage proved to bring another win for him. Aidah was a gentle wife but fiery and aggressive in bed. The proof was that ten years later they already had five children. Mahdi felt happy. All his enterprises were going well.

Their friends always pointed to them as a model family; happy, harmonious, peaceful and rich too—they did not lack anything at all.

Dark clouds entered Mahdi's life after Siau Bun Ho suddenly died of a heart attack. Mahdi felt a great loss because Siau Bun Ho was no more; Siau Bun Ho who was a quiet man, who worked hard, who had succeeded in guarding the company's finances well, supervised expenditure firmly and, with his careful attitude to management, often prevented the business from incurring various kinds of losses. Now, he was no more. Mahdi felt he should find a replacement for Siau Bun Ho quickly if their business, which was already so big, was to stay safe.

He tried a few people but they did not satisfy him and he felt his business starting to slip from his grasp. Moreover, rivals had been emerging for a while and the competition they gave was being felt more sharply.

He felt he could not maintain the business alone, and bearing in mind the interests of Siau Bun Ho's family, he suggested to them that he sell the business and explained his reasons to Bun Ho's wife. They agreed and the business was sold. Mahdi's share was large enough to provide a happy life for the rest of his days.

At first he felt content living without working. He had more time with his family and friends, not chasing around after business problems every day. But after six months he began to feel bored. He didn't have the desire to start another business.

One day when he had nothing to do, he was taken by a friend to a place where roulette was played in the Jakarta Theatre Building. Throughout his whole life, although he had always spouted his slogan—life is a game of roulette— he himself had never set foot in a place where roulette was played. He felt very attracted to it and wanted to find out about it. His friend played and he watched very carefully. His friend explained the rules.

'Ha,' said Mahdi chuckling, 'this is my game.'

He bought twenty thousand rupiahs' worth of chips and sat in the seat beside his friend. He started to play. He placed his bets listening to the words of his heart. As usual with people who have just started to gamble, he won, lost, lost, and won again. He won more than he lost. And when two hours later his friend suggested they go home because he had lost two hundred thousand rupiahs, and Mahdi counted his winnings, he was startled to see that he had won more than two hundred thousand. With a capital of twenty thousand, he was going home with more than two hundred thousand.

He laughed happily and felt he'd found a new interest and activity to fill the boredom and emptiness he had felt for the past six months. He gave his friend who had lost, one hundred thousand rupiahs. At first his friend refused it. 'No, don't,' he said, 'those are your winnings, aren't they?'

'Just take it,' Mahdi urged his friend, 'I'm only playing around. I don't really need this money that I've won.'

His friend accepted it very gratefully.

When he got home he told Aidah and his children about his experience playing roulette. They clapped their hands with delight about his winning. 'Just think,' he said to them, 'I've never played roulette in my whole life. Only today I set foot in a roulette place when I was taken by a friend who plays a lot. Yet he was the one who lost, and I, who am only a beginner, won.'

Later, when they were alone, his wife gently said to him, 'Be careful that you don't get addicted to it.'

He laughed at his wife's concern. 'Don't worry. There's no way I would become a gambling addict.'

But he did. He won and lost, won and lost, and in two years he had lost twice as much as he had won. The cash he had in savings in the bank began to dwindle. And he always went back to play saying to himself, 'Life is a game of roulette.' One roll of the ball could change a man's destiny. And if he stopped following the roll of the ball, how would his destiny be able to change? Therefore a man had to go on playing and could not stop.

And he did not stop. His relationship with his wife and children suffered and a gaping rift opened between them which grew bigger every day. After his savings in the bank had gone he began to eat into his National Development savings. Then he sold the houses that he owned, one by one, a block of land on the outskirts of the city, their cars, and finally all he had left was the house they lived in.

At this stage he met fierce opposition from his children who forced him to transfer the house to their mother's name. His wife didn't say anything, not wanting to interfere. In her heart she was very sad and sorry to see her husband's downfall. Now Mahdi could no longer find any joy in himself, or faith in his own ability, or work hard, full of conviction that he was a good husband and father. He had changed so much that in Aidah's eyes he was like a man she did not know, and would never be able to know; a man who seemed to have lost himself, who chased the miracle of a rolling ball which one day would change his destiny and bring back all his wealth to him.

Mahdi gave in and signed ownership of the house over to his wife. He knew he was finished now. He had nothing left and could no longer support his family. He never asked his wife how she was still able to put food on the table or pay the electricity and water bills. He knew the phone had been cut off a long time ago, and the food that was served had long been very plain. He did not know how his wife was still able to pay the children's school fees.

He did not know that his wife worked selling food, sold her jewellery when necessary, to continue the children's schooling, and for years had held back her tears. He did not know because there had been no communication at all between him and his wife and children for a long time.

One morning when he was having breakfast with his wife, and the children had gone to school—breakfast which they usually ate in silence—suddenly Mahdi said, 'Aidah, to-morrow I'll be going to Hong Kong. I am working again. A friend, whom I often used to help, apparently still remembers me and has asked my help in his attempt to find and buy boats in Hong Kong. I know a lot of people in shipping circles there. Here's some money he gave me in advance, two hundred thousand rupiahs. Take it.'

His wife looked at him, gave a little scream, stood up and embraced him, sobbing. His eyes filled with tears and in a low voice Mahdi said, 'Forgive me, Aidah. I have ruined all of our lives.' They embraced amidst their tears. And that night, when the whole house was quiet, for the first time in years, Mahdi held his wife and made love to her for a long time. And he gave her his word that he would stop gambling and go back to work again.

The next day he left for Hong Kong with his friend. For two weeks they were busy. Mahdi took him everywhere, in and out of offices introducing him to various businessmen who had formerly had connections with him. They were all pleased to see him again. His friend was very impressed.

After a contract to buy one ship had been signed, he said to Mahdi, 'I'm really grateful to you, Di. Thanks to you things have gone smoothly. We have to find one more ship. When that is done our work is finished. We can relax for a few days. I see you haven't lost your skill at carrying out business negotiations and approaches. If you want to be active again, I would be delighted if you would work in my company.'

'Ah, we'll talk about it later,' Mahdi said. He said it to protect his pride, but in his heart he felt happy. Two weeks later they succeeded in closing the contract for the purchase of another ship.

His friend was very happy. 'Well, Di, now we can relax. We have done what we came to do. According to our deal you get five thousand dollars. Do you want it here or in Jakarta?'

'When are we going home?'

'In four days' time. We still have an appointment with the man from Lloyd's insurance company.'

'In that case pay me one thousand here, and would you mind sending four thousand to my wife in Jakarta?'

Later that afternoon his friend invited him to visit Macao. 'I've heard a lot of stories about Macao, the last Portuguese colony in Asia,' his friend said, 'and I would like to see it before Peking takes it back again sometime.'

They set out at six in the evening and on arrival in Macao looked for a hotel straight away. At ten o'clock his friend said, 'Macao is also famous for its night-life. Let's have a walk around.'

They went in and out of bars and nightclubs and finally came to a big gambling casino. It had five storeys and each level had its own gambling game. They went from the bottom floor to the top and on the topmost floor was a roulette room. Mahdi was rather startled but he controlled himself.

'Let's play for a while,' his friend suggested. 'It doesn't matter if we throw away one or two hundred dollars.'

His friend went away to buy the chips and then sat at the

gambling table. Mahdi just stood behind him. When he saw his friend win a few times a voice inside him started to say, at first softly, but then more and more clearly, 'Life is a game of roulette,' but he hushed that voice and restrained himself.

Finally his friend lost and said, 'Oh dear, I've lost, Di. I won two hundred dollars earlier but it's gone again. What's more, my capital's all gone too.' He laughed. 'Aren't you going to play?' he asked.

'No, I promised Aidah.'

'Good for you, a husband who keeps a promise to his wife,' his friend commented.

They went back to the hotel. In bed, Mahdi lay building castles in the air of his room. In his imagination he saw the roulette room of a little while ago and he remembered his thousand dollars—'Life is a game of roulette', a small voice whispered inside him. Who knows, if he was lucky, one thousand could become fifty thousand or one hundred thousand. Why not try? He could put one thousand dollars, once, on number 36. If he won he would get his money back plus thirty-six thousand dollars, then he could put another thirty-six thousand on 36 again and if he won he would get thirty-six times thirty-six thousand. Then he would stop and go home. He would have a capital of one million, two hundred and ninety-six thousand dollars. He would recover his wealth. This would be enough capital to start a new business. He would try again. His friend had acknowledged that he hadn't lost his business skills. He still had a good approach, he could still convince other people. Ah, there was no need for him to stop at winning one million dollars. One or two million would be enough. He would invite some of his other friends into partnership. He would work hard again. He would snatch back his former life. Would he do it? Did he dare to face the spin of the roulette wheel again? If he lost, weren't four thousand dollars already safe in Jakarta with Aidah? No one need know about his loss in Macao.

And this would definitely be his last bet with the roulette ball. He fell asleep full of dreams, worry and hope.

The next morning after breakfast his friend invited him on a tourist trip to look around Macao, and after lunch suggested they go back to Hong Kong that day. 'I've had enough of Macao, Di,' he said, 'there's nothing else for us to see here.'

Seeing Mahdi hesitate, he said that if Mahdi was still liking it, he could stay another night in Macao and he would go back earlier to Hong Kong and wait for Mahdi the next day at the hotel.

And that was what they agreed to do. After taking his friend to the ferry wharf, on the way back to the hotel Mahdi felt rather worried because he had not gone back to Hong Kong with him. In his heart he grew more anxious. But when evening came, and after he had had dinner, he could no longer control the urge to go to the casino. With a pounding heart he took the lift to the top floor, to the room of the roulette tables. He spent all of his thousand dollars on chips. He inspected several tables and placed them all on number 36.

Suddenly the atmosphere around the table changed. Everyone held their breath and it was as though this was sensed by every person who was present in the room. The croupier raised his head to summon someone. He whispered to the man who came, who went away quickly and came back with another man. He examined the table and nodded his head. In the meantime people from other tables came to watch and Mahdi heard the intake of breath from every player who saw the pile of chips, 'Oooooh!'

The croupier gave the warning that the ball was about to be rolled and that anyone who wanted to place a bet should do so immediately, and then he rolled the ball. Ktak, ktak, ktak, at first it moved quickly, then slower and slower, and something heavy was felt in the room. All the spectators' attention was on the ball, making it heavy, and slower and slower, about to stop on 34, ah, still moving, slowly ... almost at 35, reaching it, oh no, number 36 will lose everything. Ah, but the ball was still moving, very slowly, slowly, it would get to 36. Mahdi sat tensely, his face pale, holding his breath, his eyes burning like the eyes of a wild animal, fixed on the ball, willing it to keep moving, ordering it to 36; and the ball moved very slowly, got to number 36 and stopped. The sound of breath that had been held and expelled from lungs filled the room. The croupier signalled to an employee standing beside him, who went off and returned bringing chips for Mahdi, thirty-six thousand dollars' worth. Within Mahdi pleasant, warm feelings arose, convincing him. This was his night, the night when the spin of the roulette wheel would change his destiny, the moment he had pursued for years.

And once again the sound of people holding their breath filled the room and now everyone who was there gathered around the table where Mahdi was playing. After getting another signal from another employee the croupier spun the wheel. The atmosphere was incredibly tense when Mahdi placed his original capital of one thousand dollars and his winnings of thirty-six thousand back on number 36.

A few people followed suit and put their bets on 36. Only the clacking sound of the rolling ball could be heard in the room. All eyes followed the ball which rolled from number to number and finally stopped on number ... 7.

'I am finished! I am ruined.'

Mahdi stood up and said good evening and walked out of the room. The people who saw him go could not guess the feelings running wild in him. Although his expression was rather tense, he seemed to walk firmly and calmly.

Mahdi went to the toilet and examined his pockets and his wallet. He was shocked, he only had fifty Hong Kong dollars left. And he remembered that he had to pay for his hotel room, because he had refused to let his friend pay. 'We're not working here,' he had said, 'but just relaxing together, so we'll pay for ourselves.' He had wanted to hold on to his pride.

It was a long time that night before he fell asleep, disturbed by dreams of the roulette ball that almost changed his life. The next morning he saw the hotel manager and asked for the hotel's understanding of his situation. He asked for a loan to get back to Hong Kong, from where he would send the money to pay the cost of his room. 'My friend is in Hong Kong,' he said.

But the hotel manager said that the hotel rules stated that any guest who did not pay had to surrender his passport, luggage and clothing and vacate the room at once, but may telephone to ask for help to redeem them.

So, he returned to his room, lay on the bed and felt very exhausted, worn out and disgusted with himself and his life. Did he have the nerve to phone his friend in Hong Kong? He didn't need much, only five hundred dollars to pay for his room and redeem his things. Why didn't he just finish his life now, his life that was worthless?

When these thoughts flashed through his mind he remembered again his whole past life. Suddenly a knock on the door was heard. The hotel bellboy had come to get his luggage. And Mahdi looked at the telephone, still unable to decide what to do.

CHAPTER TEN

The Supplier

My name is Bejo. My father, Saputro Wardono, was a senior state official. I don't need to explain his exact position. The reader can guess for himself. I had just finished Senior High School when my uncle, Sumadi, invited me to set up something called a *rekanan* business with him. It had never entered my head to go into business. I was still enjoying school and going around with girls. I thought business was something difficult. But my uncle reminded me that for a person like me, with a father like mine, everything would be easy. But a *rekanan* business? 'I don't understand *rekanan*, Uncle.'

'Its meaning in English is "supplier",' my uncle said, explaining.

'I don't understand that either. As far as I remember I've never heard that word in Mrs Martono's English lessons. What is a "supplier", Uncle?' I asked again.

Uncle looked at me in surprise. 'You have graduated from Senior High School and you don't even know the meaning of the English word "supplier"?' he said in astonishment.

'No, I don't, Uncle.'

'A supplier is a business that sells goods or equipment needed by other businesses,' he said.

'Oh,' I replied, '*rekanan* is the same as supplier and you and I are going to open a supplier business.'

'Oh, you are clever,' Uncle said happily.

Uncle had a lot more to say about profits and profit-sharing, and he had visions of how we would all get rich quickly and be able to do whatever we wanted to. Then he told me to discuss the plan with my mother and then let her tell my father. If they both agreed then he would go ahead.

'Why don't you just tell Mother and Father yourself?' I asked.

'You are stupid,' he said. 'Didn't I tell you just now that this idea should appear to come from you? You tell them you want to be a businessman and they can help. If they ask who is going to assist you, only then mention my name. Tell your mother you've only stopped studying temporarily, and will go back to it again in two or three years' time. And tell her this is the last chance for us all, especially her, to get rich and not be outdone by her friends and other relatives. The opportunity should not be missed while your father is still in such a high position. Remind your mother to look at Aunty Sriyana. Her husband has become the director of a bank. How rich she is! And Aunty Kartini's husband is Director of Krakatau Steel. My god, she's rich. She's got fifty imported dogs! Doesn't your mother want to be like them? How long will your father be such a high official?'

I hadn't expected that mother would agree so easily and quickly. I was worried that she would object and order me to go on with my studies.

'Let me fix it up with your father,' Mother said. And more surprising to me was how Father also quickly and immediately agreed. What's more, after Mother spoke with him, he called me in and praised me for having such an idea.

'Bejo,' Father said, 'I am happy to have a son like you. You have just finished school and you've already got big ideas. That's what a young man should be like. You can get on with that sort of spirit. You can continue with your studies later if you still want to. But if you have money, lack of education is no problem. With money you can buy the brains of clever people.'

Father laughed, 'Ha ha ha,' and I laughed too, 'Ha ha ha,' and so did Mother, 'Ha, ha, ha, ha.'

'I had begun to worry that we would not be able to take advantage of my position, because you seemed to be only interested in chasing girls. I almost asked your mother to establish a business. You know, all my colleagues have businesses as suppliers for various state authorities and enterprises. What's more, many of them have not been backward in getting their wives to become directors of their companies. I don't think that's so good. It's too blatant in the eyes of the public. That's not good policy. But if you and your uncle set up a business, that's your right. You, my son, and your uncle, your mother's young brother, have the right to your own lives.

'Tell your uncle to get ready quickly and draw up an official document for establishing a company. In the coming three months many tenders will be opened for all kinds of goods and equipment. Later I'll give you the necessary lists and show you the way to arrange the prices. I don't see any problems. But your company must have an office and telephone and must be seen to have convincing prestige. Then you'll get orders not for tens of thousands of rupiahs, or one or two million, but hundreds of millions, perhaps several billion.'

Happily I reported back to Uncle and in a week a notarial document was finished and the notary said that the company could begin operating. The ratification from the Ministry of Justice would follow later; he would arrange it.

The second week, Uncle took me to start work in the office. The office proved to be a room which was not very big, but situated in a multi-storeyed building on Sudirman Avenue. A servant, a messenger and a female secretary with an attractive figure had already been employed. The office space was divided into three; the secretary's area, which was also the place where guests reported, a small room to receive them, and another room with three desks and two iron cupboards. The office seemed to me to be presentable enough, although I felt it was still too empty. But we had just started, hadn't we?

'Who is the other desk for, Uncle?' I asked.

Uncle smiled. 'Sit down first, that's your desk at the end there. How does it feel to be a director of Mercu Angkasa Pty. Ltd., huh? Is it nice?'

'It doesn't feel nice yet, Uncle,' I said. 'There is no money in my pocket yet, I don't have a car, and I don't know what I have to do.'

'Be patient, be patient,' he said, laughing. That uncle of mine was certainly a funny man. He laughed at anything. 'Wait for our partner, the other director. The money is coming from him.'

An hour later our partner had not come. Uncle had started to get restless. Two hours later he still hadn't come. Several times Uncle got Aisah, the secretary, to ring him at his home but they said he'd been gone since morning. Because there was nothing to do, I went and sat in the front room and chatted with Aisah. Ah, I was beginning to feel how nice it was to be a boss. Whatever I said, Aisah nodded and agreed with.

'Would you like us to have lunch together later?'

She nodded in agreement.

'What if we go to the movies after work?'

She wanted that too.

'Hmm,' I thought to myself, 'if this is what it's like, it's good working as a director.'

Uncle called me inside. 'Hey, Bejo,' he said, 'during office hours, don't bother the female employees. If you want to go around with them that's all right, but do it outside office hours.'

'Oh, is that business rules, Uncle?' I asked.

'Yes,' he said, 'you have a lot to learn first. If you get familiar in the office the work can suffer. Outside the office it's up to you.'

'Right, Uncle, I'll remember. OK, boss,' I said, and Uncle laughed again.

According to the notarial document, Uncle was director number one, I was director number two and our partner, a

Chinese, was director number three. But I thought the one with most power was actually my mother, because she held the office of Commissioner President, while two of my younger brothers who were still very small, four and six years old respectively, were the other two commissioners. According to the notarial document which the notary read to us at the signing, my mother, as the commissioner president, had the right if she felt it was necessary for the good of the company, to hold office on the board of directors, separately or simultaneously with her post as commissioner.

And in the course of one month my mother was required to call an extraordinary meeting of shareholders to present final decisions on her actions. Because my mother, my two brothers and I together held fifty-one per cent of all the shares, and Uncle and our partner, what's his name again, I had only seen him twice, Bintang something or other, held forty-nine per cent, the company was actually controlled by my mother. And because my mother controlled it, it meant too, that the company was fully controlled by my father. It was really a very good system, wasn't it? I felt there was really no need to have any doubts about dedicating myself to the progress of Mercu Angkasa Pty. Ltd., because all the advances of the company also meant the advance of my family. I mean my family's progress in the field of finance. This was important. We all need money, the more the better, for the sake of happiness, don't we?

Not long afterwards Bintang arrived, very apologetic to Uncle and me because he was late. Meanwhile Father had handed over a long, thick list of tenders for various kinds of large and small equipment, materials, goods and so on required by the state-owned Permata Oil Co.

'Right,' Uncle said, 'let's go to the conference room to discuss this. Bintang, we have to hurry if we want to win these tenders. We have to choose the right ones, two or three very big ones, but we really have to be able to hand over the goods. If this first time our work is satisfactory, then it will be easy from now on. We'll have an easy life, and we can expand our efforts and become suppliers to other government authorities. As you know, for every tender we have to supply guarantee money—the term in the world language of suppliers is "performance bond". We must provide capital for that, and it's also usual for there to be capital to entertain the big shots—the term is "entertainment fund". Because as soon as we put in tenders, then all kinds of requests will come from the gentlemen who arrange things on the inside. They will ask to be treated to massage parlours, to tickets to watch football matches, tickets to Singapore and Hong Kong and other kinds of tickets.'

'Yes, yes,' Bintang said, 'don't worry.' His name was Indonesian, it's true—'Bintang'—but his Indonesian language was still far from the good Indonesian taught in school and desired by Mr Yus Badudu on television. Moreover, I thought this Bintang was still thoroughly Chinese. But yes, the capital was coming from him. 'That's nothing,' he said to Uncle, 'there are many of them who ask to be lented a loom for a bel weekend on Putli Island or at Ancol, with the contents supplied. You understand what I mean, don't you, Mr Bejo?'

I was startled to be called 'Mr'. I'd never been called 'Mr' in my life. Apparently if we became directors we went on and became misters. Aisah was right when she addressed me as 'sir' earlier. How could this be? I didn't have any children or a wife, and now I'd become a 'Mr'. It felt very funny, this being a director. From now on I am writing Bintang's defective pronunciation in accordance with correct Indonesian spelling. It's not pleasant seeing 'r' become 'l' in my manuscript. Aren't these my first memoirs? The others will follow later. Provided the reader just knows that our partner was still thoroughly Chinese and his Indonesian was still thoroughly Chinese Indonesian.

'Eh, what's that?' I asked, because Bintang and Uncle were looking at me.

'It's like this, Mr Bejo,' Bintang said, 'if later on the gentlemen ask for girls, you arrange it and I'll give you the money.'

'Heavens,' I replied, 'I don't know any of those sort of girls. If we boys at high school wanted girls like that we never paid for them. Where do I look for them, Mr Bintang?'

'It's all easy. Later on I'll give you an album with addresses and telephone numbers. It's all been arranged.'

Well, I got very interested. 'Where's the album?' I asked.

'Later, later. Now let's have a good look at the list first.'

He and Uncle read the list carefully and discussed various technical matters that I didn't understand. I just let them work, while my thoughts were still on the album, phone numbers and addresses. I felt that this job of director had become more interesting. How pleased Mother would be to hear of this job of mine.

But looking at me, Uncle could read my thoughts and he said, 'Bejo, the matter of the album and the special services to the gentlemen are company secrets and may not be revealed to outsiders, especially your mother. It would be a disaster for us all. The commissioner president would close down the company.'

'Ah, if we have to keep company secrets, of course I can, too. OK, boss,' I said.

After three hours of discussion we finally reached an agreement to offer large equipment to Permata. Bintang would provide the necessary capital.

'Provided we get a letter from your father, Mr Bejo, stating that we will definitely win the tender, the money is a minor matter. Everyone is prepared to give a loan, provided it's for profit,' Bintang said.

Apparently Father was not prepared to sign such a letter. 'Call that Chinese of yours and tell him to come to the house,' Father said. 'Fancy fooling around with letters like that. Does he want to implicate me? Where did your uncle find him? Bring him to the house tomorrow, very early.'

Bintang arrived early in the morning and was immediately reprimanded by Father. 'If you want to make money now-adays, you have to be smart, and not leave any traces.'

I was proud to see my father instructing and reprimanding a big time Chinese wheeler-dealer like Bintang. 'I guaranteed that the Mercu Angkasa Company would win the tender, what more do you want? Don't you trust me?'

'I trust you, sir, I trust you,' said Bintang, 'it's my friend who needs the letter.'

'You bring him here and I'll talk to him,' Father said.

The upshot was that Father did not sign a letter, we put in our tender and the guarantee money was paid in full. And I was busy with the album, phone numbers and addresses. It was certainly a very valuable lesson in life for me. Later I want to say a lot about my job as director, with the albums, phone numbers and addresses, serving the gentlemen. But I don't want this report of mine to become a porno story. Readers can imagine for themselves what can happen when a young man, freshly graduated from high school, gets such a job as a company director ... hmm.

Waiting for the day of the announcement of who was going to win the tender, Uncle and Bintang began to get anxious, especially Bintang. I could understand it because if our tender didn't win, it was Bintang who was going to lose money.

I had no doubts at all. I had begun to enjoy the pleasures of being a director. I'd been given a company car by Bintang, and although it wasn't the Mercedes sports that I longed for, but a Honda Civic, that was all right for a start. But as soon as our tender won I was going to press my uncle and Bintang to buy me a Mercedes sports. A young director like me had to look after his prestige, didn't he?

When only a few days remained before the date when the winner of the tender was announced, and Bintang heard a rumour that it was a South Korean firm that was said to have put out ten thousand dollars to smooth the way to winning, the atmosphere in the office of Mercu Angkasa Pty. Ltd. was very chilly, at least several degrees below zero, and the neon light that lit the office was also dim, not bright as usual. Aisah also seemed worried. Perhaps she was frightened the office would be forced to close down and she would have to go and so she would be separated from me, the one who always invited her to discotheques and sometimes took her to enjoy the beauty of the coast at Ancol under the beautiful full moon. Not for a long time, don't get the wrong idea. Even though I rented a bungalow there for the night, we only ever stayed one or two hours at the most. And I took her there properly and returned her politely to her father and mother.

Perhaps Aisah's parents considered me as their prospective son-in-law, but I felt that as long as Aisah worked for our company, and as long as I was a director, it was not possible for me to marry her. After all, Uncle had already reminded me that a director must not play around with his secretary during office hours, let alone marry her—right?

'What does your father say, Mr Bejo?' Bintang kept asking me.

'Look,' I said, 'hasn't he already promised? It's sure to be all arranged, why make a fuss like this? Look at me, I'm not making a fuss, am I? I'm not worried. Calm down, just calm down, Mr Bintang, you must settle down.'

But I telephoned Mother anyway and reported the atmosphere of restlessness and depression in the office and said that as commissioner president it would be good if she did something with ... ah, she knew, didn't she?

'I think everything has been settled,' Mother said. 'Yesterday, he, you know who I mean, don't you?'

'Yes, boss,' I answered.

'Right, well, yesterday the boss still told me that it was all settled. Why are they so anxious?'

'Oh, I've already told them all that, Mother. "Look at me," I said to them, "am I not calm like a director should be?" Isn't that right, Mother? But,' and I lowered my voice, 'Bintang has outlaid a few million, hasn't he?'

'Ah, that's nothing, he's just got the gripes,' Mother said, 'and they say he's a big operator! Just wait, I'll fix it with the boss.'

I immediately told Uncle and Bintang the good news that the president would take action at once, and that yesterday Father had given her another guarantee that everything was all right. 'And which father would dare to fool around with the president of Mercu Angkasa Pty. Ltd.?' I said. 'Just be calm, Mr Bintang,' I said, 'and don't forget when the tender is settled, a Mercedes sports for me, right?'

'When it's settled, eh, when it's settled,' Mr Bintang said, 'you'll be able to get more than a Mercedes sports, Mr Bejo!'

'Well that's right, we'll have this big business,' I said.

I was surprised that my uncle, who was usually such a good talker, now joined in the tension and uneasiness with Bintang, and since the morning had hardly said a word. Ah, perhaps he was worried like Aisah was too, that if the company failed to win the tender, it would possibly have to be closed down and he would lose his directorship. He would go back to being unemployed or being a village schoolteacher in Kasongan village outside Yogyakarta. Of course, this was not a bright picture of the future for Uncle. In Jakarta lately he had started to get used to life in restaurants, hotels and international offices. Going back to Kasongan village, which was arid in all respects, would naturally be hard. I understood his feelings.

Whereas I didn't need to worry about anything at all, did I? Uncle had a family of eight children. I was still single. The worst that could happen to me would be having to go back to study if Mercu Angkasa Pty. Ltd. failed.

But after I reported my telephone conversation with the commissioner president, Uncle and Bintang seemed to cheer up again. Tomorrow seemed brighter to them, and apparently bright enough for them to see that it was already ten past one.

'That's enough now, don't think about it any more,' Bintang said. "Let's have lunch now.'

'Well, that's right,' I said, 'whatever happens, even if Mercu Angkasa loses tens of millions of rupiahs, we still have to go on eating.' And I laughed. I meant to cheer them up, but their faces dropped again. Apparently my two director friends didn't think my joke was funny.

'Yes,' I said to myself, 'everyone has his own sense of humour. What makes one person laugh can make someone else angry or even sad.'

I had a very delicious lunch that day, you know, my stomach was very hungry. But Uncle and Bintang picked at their food as though they'd bitten their own tongues. Poor things.

But apparently the big boss, my father, was not all talk. Our tender won! Oh, the reader who has never been a big businessman like me, of course will not be able to feel how exciting it is for one who wins a tender after working hard for months, and facing competition from home and abroad. Among the rivals that we defeated there were even giant multinational companies.

For me, especially, our victory had its own significance. Because I was very aware, that as a company director of only a few months, I had no experience at all, but I had taken part in helping to win the tender so gloriously. Winning the second tender and so on would certainly be easier for me. Now I had control of the albums, phone numbers and addresses, including of course, those whose photos were in the albums. Naturally, my services to the gentlemen would be more satisfactory. When I began I was still green in these matters. But now, ah, I don't like to brag about myself, but I can humbly say that I had experience too. Of course, not yet as much as the big time gentlemen, but enough.

Bintang was ecstatic. So was Uncle. And the president

was, too. And so was the big boss himself. We had a party to celebrate. Blessings and praise to those in authority who had given fortune like this, cheaply, to us all!

Six months after our tender won I returned the Honda Civic to the office and now I drove my Mercedes sports. It was only fitting, I felt, for a successful director like me. And this car was in my own name. It was not the firm's car. A lot of my friends used to like parading in their fathers' Mercedes Tigers, but they were cars belonging to their fathers' firms. This belonged to me. There wasn't a girl who could refuse if I invited her to get in, and once they were in the car, anything could happen. The proof was Aisah. One week I invited her to Puncak and was she surprised! So were her parents. Aisah's parents who had always been so kind to me were now one hundred times kinder. If before they called me 'young lad', after they saw my luxurious Mercedes sports they called me 'young sir'. Fancy prospective in-laws calling me 'young sir'!

To cut a long story short, from then on Mercu Angkasa Pty. Ltd. never lost a tender. The money we made! Oh, if I talked about how much it would soon be thought I was putting on airs and telling lies. There was so much, it was incredible. Think of it, because I have now been a director for three years, I have wide experience, no less than other businessmen who plunged into this businessmen's world earlier than I did.

What's more, with all modesty I can say that concerning expertise in entrepreneurship, a term which I never learnt at high school previously but have only heard since I became a director, perhaps I am superior to them. I hear stories that many of them have been in business for ten or twenty years but nevertheless are incapable of advancing their business. Yet we, who only started up three years ago, had now become a major company—it could even be said a multinational because we had offices in Hong Kong, Singapore and Tokyo. But we were good businessmen. Although our company had now achieved a trade turnover of billions of dollars a year, oh sorry, a slip of the tongue, I meant billions of rupiahs a year, we did not show off and have big offices and a large staff and hundreds of employees. This is the main mistake that many Indonesian businessmen make. They are too infatuated with wanting to be seen as big businessmen, and then they have big, luxurious offices and hundreds of employees. If it's not in proportion with the size of the business then this means that the daily business costs—the term is 'overheads'—it's starting to be apparent, isn't it, that I am not just a figurehead director like lots of others, but really an active one?—then the overheads become too high and the company makes losses. If this situation is allowed to continue, the company fails, especially if the traffic of money in and out—the term is 'cash flow'—is not carefully guarded and supervised. This all requires knowledge and a large will to work, and believe me, being a successful businessman is really not easy. But providing there is the will, of course you can succeed. I'm the example of that.

When we first started Mercu Angkasa Pty. Ltd. it was with non-existent capital. Of course I have to admit that there was Bintang, the Chinese financier, with his capital, but that would certainly not have been enough without my hard work. Now I can see that what decided everything was my work with the album and so on. Of course, the presence of the boss, I mean my father, in his position also helped a bit. But you can't blame me for being the son of my father who was in a high position. That was just a coincidence, wasn't it? There are businessmen who are successful and become big without having VIP fathers as I did. For example, like Dasaat did.

To invite and attract the interest of other young men so that hordes of them enter the business world, I want to say a little now about our wealth three years after being in business, and working hard. It's not that I want to boast, but I really, sincerely want to urge Indonesian youth to plunge into business. Our society has done too much complaining that native Indonesians still belong to the low economy social class. We are always getting disgruntled and angry to see the Chinese or their descendants with more hold on the strong economic positions. We close our eyes to the fact that Indonesia does not have an indigenous middle class forming a basis for the stability of our society. Our middle class is held by the Chinese or their descendants and foreigners. Well, the only solution is for our youth to go into the business world.

Whoever wants to work hard in the world of business will be rewarded many times over. Look at us. For the past year I've had no interest any more in counting my money in the bank or in my pocket. I treat my friends to meals, sit around a lot in international hotels, spending one or two hundred thousand rupiahs doesn't worry me at all, and I'm already bored with overseas trips. I even get bored sometimes seeing girls. Too many and too often and just now I feel they don't seem special. That's why I am very selective now. If they're not one hundred per cent perfect, I don't want them any more. Take Aisah, for example; I never bother her any more, not in the office during working hours, nor for a long time now, outside office hours.

I have bought two houses in an area popular with foreigners. Mother advised me to do that. She said that if there is excess money it's better to buy houses, land or gold, and not to pile up cash. Because I am still single, I prefer living at my parents' house. I can't be bothered running my own home. Because of that I let the houses I own to foreigners. One is rented for two thousand dollars a month, paid in cash two years in advance. Well, imagine for yourself how much that is.

If the commissioner president told about the increase in her wealth, well, perhaps her story would be longer than mine. It's enough for me to say that she possibly owns the biggest diamond in Indonesia now, umpteen carats in weight. Maybe there are only one or two people who own bigger ones, but I very much doubt it. And the boss, I mean my father, hm, I know how much he's got because his share is handed over via me. But I don't feel I need to say much about the boss. It's usual all over the world, isn't it, for the boss to always get the most.

My latest project is opening a cattle-raising farm—the term is 'ranch'. This is specifically a partnership between me, the boss and the commissioner president. We succeeded in buying a neglected plantation in Central Java. I have ordered two hundred head of cattle from Australia. Our plan in the coming two years is to raise at least three thousand head. I've also ordered a start on planting two large hills with ten thousand top quality clove trees. Superior cattle, superior cloves, everything superior, that's what we have to achieve in the world of business. Don't chase after just anything, but if you are in business, go after the best quality. This is the key to success. Believe me, this is my own experience.

Uncle, yes I almost forgot to tell about Uncle. Because he is truly a village man, he always thinks of his village and wants to be buried there. Although he has a fine and beautiful house in a residential area—the term is 'real estate'—it's called Permata Hijau—he built another luxurious house in Kasongan village and he has also taken over more than ten hectares of the people's land there. Uncle doesn't seem to have the strong spirit of a businessman, er, entrepreneur. Going into business in Jakarta for him was only to increase capital. He said one day that when he had one million rupiahs he would leave Jakarta and resign from the business. He said that for him and Aunty, life in a big city like Jakarta was all noise and dirt and everyone was always in a hurry and competition was too fierce. He would prefer to live quietly in the village and just be an ordinary farmer.

Fancy Uncle saying he wanted to be an ordinary farmer, when he has a house with AC electricity, a big swimming-pool, its own electric diesel, tractors, a deluxe sedan car and hired farm labourers! A wealthy farmer is what he will be. And Bintang didn't miss out on his share. It's surprising how little effect so much money had on him. He is just like he was before; he hasn't changed. He still buys his clothes at the market where a seamstress makes them. Whereas I myself fit out my wardrobe in Paris, London, Rome and New York. Once you've worn silk shirts made in Italy then you don't want to wear Arrow or Manhattan brand shirts made in Tanah Abang any more. I buy my trousers and jackets at the Lanvin shop in Paris or New York and my shoes in Rome. It won't be long before I'm on the list of best dressed men and women in 1981, 1982, 1983 and so on.

I feel sorry for my friends who are still content to wear blue jeans and baggy shirts. Poor things, they don't know what it's like to have clothes which are better and more prestigious.

There is another free lesson which I must give to the youth of my generation who want to enter the world of business: prestige; prestige must always be maintained. Invite your business clients to first class restaurants. If you travel by car it must still be the most luxurious car. Although if money is really short, just rent a Mercedes Tiger for an hour. It's no problem. Don't be seen getting into a beaten up blue or yellow heap of a taxi to go to a business meeting which will discuss projects to the value of hundreds of millions or billions of dollars. How would people have confidence in you?

While our supplier business was progressing fast and incalculable amounts of money were coming in, at a direc-tors' meeting we decided to expand the business into other fields—in business terminology, 'diversification'. We set up a collective company to establish a cement factory in South Sumatra, a large oil palm plantation in Lampung, a big cotton plantation in Flores and a car assembly plant in Tanjung Priok. The cars of course were Japanese cars which were very much in demand. At first we tried to take over an agency for Mitsubishi Colts which were so popular, but finding one was a bit difficult. Father said it didn't matter, we would try again next year. But we got the agency for a new Japanese model which could use natural gas. This will surely surprise everyone later. Just wait for the date it's released.

As an honest reporter, I must also confess that in the business world we have to be lucky too. If we are lucky, what is certain, as I have already explained several times, is that this must be accompanied by hard, honest and responsible work, and then everything can succeed. But if there is no luck, even if we have worked hard and responsibly with all honesty, then our business can fail anyway. But don't be broken-hearted, don't give up hope. Our business also met failure a few times, for example, when we wanted to get into clove importing. Goodness, it was really hard. The big boss himself was not able to change anything at all in the very profitable clove trade. That was one of our big failures. What's more, Bintang and I worked hard within Indonesia and spent a lot of money, and we also wasted a lot of time and money going to Madagascar to look for clove suppliers there. Our second failure was when we tried to implement our new project, a flour factory for the whole of Sumatra. We had bought the land at Belawan, at a port. The roads had been built and a wharf specially for ships which carried wheat from the United States had also been installed. But when our side was all ready, apparently the permit which had been promised could not be given and we were told to wait another year or two. Well, for me, this was quite a bitter lesson.

Nevertheless we did not despair or give up hope. Another thing we failed at was winning the Datsun Agency. You will remember when the quarrel occurred between the Japanese

Marubeni Company and its Indonesian partner, with the result that the Japanese stopped sending cars to be assembled in Indonesia. There were many groups around including our company, that wanted to take over the position of 'X' Pty. Ltd. who were the original partners of the Japanese. God, as a rational businessman I felt sick to see tens of millions wasted just on holding discussions—the right term is 'lobbying'. Because we are modern businessmen we lobbied not only in Jakarta, but as far away as Tokyo. I got to the stage of being sick of eating sukiyaki as a result of all the lobbying I had to do in Tokyo with Bintang.

After months and months of working hard like that in Jakarta and Tokyo the result was—zero. But I did not despair. This all had to be a lesson and an incentive to work even harder, even better.

Well, now I come to our last and biggest failure. We decided to save our company, which had suffered severe blows, by entering the international gold market in London. If we were successful it would be a national and international sensation.

We went in, in a big way, staking everything when the price of gold was moving up. I will not mention here how many million dollars we invested in the gold market, but we really only followed in the footsteps of the Bank of Indonesia.

'We will buy gold the same as the Bank of Indonesia does,' we thought. 'What's good for them must also be good for Mercu Angkasa Pty. Ltd.'

It turned out that after we bought, the price of gold had reached its highest level, and the next day the price did not move up any more as it had been doing in the preceding weeks. At first I wasn't worried. Gold would surely keep going up. Who in the world would be stupid and want to hold on to paper money these days? But instead of going up, on the contrary, it started to fall, and set off another panic.

'Hayaaa, it's a dreadful disaster, terrible,' Mr Bintang kept shouting.

Uncle was as he always was if there was a critical situation: he just sat and kept quiet and looked surly. Disaster—the price of gold kept falling. In an atmosphere of panic and misery, finally a meeting of directors decided to sell the gold again as quickly as possible before the loss got worse.

I do not need to mention how much we lost. Just thinking of it could give me a heart attack. And then came the calamity. The big boss had given the signal that Permata was going to open a huge tender for tanker-ships. Whoever could supply the various-sized tankers first, would get the order.

How busy we were with it! This was our chance to recover from the blow of the gold market. And I imagined one day becoming the Onassis of South-East Asia.

We borrowed money from the bank, because a wise businessman will not use his own money to carry out his business but will always use borrowed bank money. A phone call from the big boss gave his personal support to the director of the relevant bank and everything was organized. We paid an advance deposit for a number of ships and put in our tender in accordance with the regulations in force.

And we waited. Mr Bintang and Uncle kept on counting the profits that would come in. They told me that if we won, not only would the losses on the gold market be covered, but we would all be richer than we had ever been before. Well, that's the lot of a businessman. If you are above wind everything is terrific, if you are being hit, your stomach heaves up and down. You have to hang on, as I've already said.

Waiting for the decision to come out was always enjoyable, because my special job was looking after the important gentlemen. And as a host I also had to meet them and see that they were really happy and relaxed. Whatever they tasted, I had to taste first because I felt full responsibility for this work.

So two months passed quickly, full of pleasure for me. But on a certain day suddenly there was panic in the office again.

Our name did not come forth as the winner. Moreover, the winner was another company that was not well known. And two days later I read in the paper that the big boss had been honourably discharged by the government from his very important office, with many thanks for all his services in carrying out his duties to the nation and the people.

And does the reader know who won; who was behind this new company? None other than Bambang, the oldest son of the new big shot who replaced my father. Do not forget this lesson, reader. In the world nowadays the old proverb still applies—when the *sirih* has lost its sweetness, it is thrown away.

Mother was furious with the people who sacked Father, but he said, 'Leave it alone, Mother, that's the way things are in this life. If we are in favour and needed we are used, if we are no longer needed we are tossed out just like that. There's no need to worry, we won't go short of anything.'

It was all right for Father to talk like that. But it was Uncle and Bintang and I who had to swallow the bitterness. Because a few months later Mercu Angkasa Pty. Ltd. and all its subsidiaries starting from the oil palm plantation, the cement factory, the car assembly and so on, were no longer able to pay their interest, let alone pay off any of the debts to our creditor banks. All of the funds from these businesses had been tapped before to go into the gold trade and to provide capital to buy the tankers. All the advance money paid to buy the tankers had been wasted.

The loss of all this was actually not a problem to me. Go ahead, the banks could take it all. I still had quite a large personal fortune.

But what worried me were stories in the newspaper that said that the Attorney-General was considering investigating various supplier companies in Indonesia that were suspected of using bribery to win tenders in state-owned companies and government authorities and working in league with persons in those companies and authorities.

Yes, this is what made me feel uneasy. And two days later,

when a letter from the Attorney-General arrived at the office brought directly by a prosecutor, summoning the members of the board of directors of Mercu Angkasa Pty. Ltd. and clearly stating Uncle's name, then Bintang's and my own, suddenly I shook as though I had fever, I felt weak in the knees, my stomach went cold and bilious and my heart pounded.

I did not feel at all guilty of violating a particular law in our country. If I was later charged with corruption, what was wrong about that? If I'm not mistaken, don't I recall that the late Mr Hatta himself admitted that corruption had become part of the way of life in our country? Were we guilty if we acted in accordance with the conventions of our own society?

We had a discussion and decided before facing the prosecutor, to consult with a legal expert. He said that perhaps administrative mistakes had been made, for example, using bank credit for purposes other than those presented to the bank when asking for credit. And concerning the charges of bribery and inciting civil servants and officers to carry out corrupt practices—the term is 'commercialization of office' —'You don't need to fear, sirs,' our clever lawyer said. 'If all the cases of corruption, big and small, were prosecuted, then perhaps there would be no more Indonesians living out of jail,' he joked. I felt his joke was inappropriate because hearing the word 'jail', my heart pounded and I felt quite sick. I was seized with fear and I held my breath. But then he soothed my feelings by saying, 'Supposing, and this is supposing in capital letters, sirs, the Attorney-General charged you with corruption and with corrupting officers, there's no need to worry too much because I am used to arranging a solution of problems with the judges.'

'Well, here is a real lawyer.' I wasn't aware that any words had come out of my mouth, but they were smiling. Bintang paid him a million rupiahs in cash as an advance for handling the possibility of all kinds of matters awaiting us, and only then did I feel a bit better.

That night I felt the need to console myself. Mother had

disappeared looking confused and frightened and Father did not come out of his room. I phoned Lili to invite her to dinner and a disco. 'No,' she said, 'another time. I have to study. I have an exam tomorrow at the university.'

'All right, if you want to be a bookworm student it's up to you,' I thought. Karina couldn't come either. After I had made twelve phone calls to my friends who all this time as soon as they heard my voice would speak softly and full of the hot breath of love, I started to get suspicious. And two hours later, when I had phoned I don't know how many girls who used to run and chase me when I whistled, I was convinced that they were scared to be seen with me because of the scandal that had struck our company and the big boss being honourably discharged.

Together, the three of us faced the prosecutor in the Attorney-General's office. I felt worried when we were separated and questioned in separate rooms by a prosecutor—the term is 'interrogation'.

After one hour's interrogation, asking my name, when and where I was born, who were my parents, what was my job and so on, the prosecutor said that he had orders to detain me for purposes of investigation.

'There is no need to worry, sir,' he added, 'this is only temporary. When the investigation is finished of course you will be released again.'

'What about Uncle, eh, the other directors?' I asked, with difficulty preventing my voice from shaking.

'It's the same for them too,' he answered briefly.

So, I am writing this report in a detention room of the prosecutor's office, as a lesson for all of the younger generation of Indonesia.

Do not give up hope. Justice will prevail. I am trying to cheer myself up waiting to be taken in front of the court.

I have started to feel optimistic because our lawyer has come and seen me.

'Don't be afraid, Mr Bejo,' he said, 'many other bigger corruptors than you are free.'

CHAPTER ELEVEN

Broken Glass

DOCTOR KOO TIO SWAN said good night to his last patient and closed and locked the door to his office. His assistant had gone home at 10 o'clock, three hours ago. He leant against the door for a moment, closed his eyes and took a very deep breath, stretching his muscles. He let out his feeling of exhaustion. He was a popular doctor and very much liked by his patients. During the day he worked at the army hospital and later, starting from four in the afternoon, he practised at his home until all hours of the night, depending on the number of patients who came. He didn't have the heart to fix a final hour for his practice to be open for patients in the evenings. He felt he could not tell the patients who came, to come back the next day because opening hours were finished. Sick people must be helped, that was his opinion. In the end very often he had to work till 11 p.m., 12, or 1 a.m. His wife had for a long time scolded him, frightened he would get sick because he worked too hard.

'It would be tolerable if you were getting a lot of income working like that,' his wife reproached him, 'like other doctors do. If you get sick you'll know it. There are limits to a man's strength.'

'I am a doctor, Mai,' he said to his wife, 'as long as people come to ask for my help I have an obligation to give it to them.'

'I know,' she said, 'but why don't you do what other doctors do and use a number system to limit the number of patients who come each day? Twenty people or however

many is appropriate so that you can finish no later than 8 or
9 o'clock at night. Think of yourself a bit. And what about
us—your wife and five children who almost never see their
father? Boy is eight years old now; when did you last take
him and his young brothers and sisters for a holiday or a
picnic? And Salina who used to often play chess with you,
you've not played with her for at least five years. Don't
children also need the love and attention of their father?'

Tio remembered when he was a child in Malang. His
childhood had been very happy because there were just him
and his younger sister. His mother and father spoiled the
two of them very much, and his grandfather and grand-
mother even more so. Nevertheless, he smiled remembering
his father disciplining them when it was necessary. He and
his sister grew up in the embrace and shelter of their parents
and their family. His father, Koo Thay Wie, was a rich
trader, and two or three generations before him Indonesian
blood had entered the Koo family. He and his sister were
not sent to a Chinese school, but a Dutch one. They went to
Dutch Elementary School, then to HBS. At home they did
not speak Chinese either. His parents themselves could no
longer speak it well. His teenage years passed in the happiness and joy of youth. He himself had lots of Dutch and
Indonesian friends. During the years before the outbreak of
World War II, before the Japanese army invaded Indonesia,
he was not touched by the Indonesian struggle for national
independence. He heard a lot about this from his Indonesian
friends who talked with great spirit about Soekarno, Hatta,
Sjahrir, Sarikat Islam, Communism, *cultuurstelsel*, the system
of forced planting carried out by the Dutch colonial power
squeezing the people, and about how they had to struggle to
free the Indonesian people and homeland from the Dutch.
He heard from his friends and read in the newspapers about
the oath of Indonesian Youth: one language, one nation, one
flag—the Red and White. He also read about places where
the Dutch disposed of political prisoners, in Tanah Merah,

Boven Digul, places full of malaria and places where many
Indonesian political prisoners died. But none of this touched
him. He finished HBS not long after the Japanese army
landed in Java. The years of the Japanese occupation were
years full of worry for their family. Their parents always
warned them to be careful, and avoid the Japanese soldiers
as much as possible. He saw his Dutch friends disappear
into Japanese concentration camps. He saw his young Indonesian friends full of activity in various movements supporting the Japanese slogan to build the Great All Asia Co-
Prosperity Sphere. And he heard and read a lot more about
Soekarno, Hatta and Sjahrir.

Sometimes he felt there was something calling him to
involve himself in some of the things going on around him,
but for some reason he never felt himself impelled to do so.

Their family was safe during the years of Japanese occupation, and when Soekarno and Hatta proclaimed Indonesian independence he was in Yogyakarta attending to his
father's business.

He felt drawn to staying in Yogyakarta. The main motiv-
ation for this was because in Yogyakarta he fell in love with
Mai Ling, a girl of Chinese descent who had in her the
beauty of a mixture of Chinese and Indonesian blood;
Indonesian gentleness and Chinese perseverance and indus-
try. He felt quite bewitched by Mai, and three months after
they met they were married. His parents came from Malang
for the wedding. During the years of the revolution they
lived simply. The war against the Dutch colonial army
almost immobilized his father's business. Mai, who proved
to be an expert on women's clothing, opened a dressmaking
business at home and thus they got to know many of the
wives of the leaders and officials of the Government of the
Republic of Indonesia in Yogyakarta.

One day an Indonesian official who had become his friend
said to him, 'Tio,' (he had not changed his name for an
Indonesian one), 'you are still young, you are a graduate of

HBS, what business can you do while the war against the Dutch is going on like this? Why don't you finish your studies? You said your ambition was to be a doctor.'

'Where is there a medical school nowadays?' Tio asked in reply.

'Instead of wasting time like this, why don't you go to Holland to study?'

He was startled. At first he felt frightened, worrying that his friend was testing him. But then his friend added, 'If you are interested, in two days' time I am going to Jakarta with a group of Republicans. You can come with us. From Jakarta you can leave for Holland. There are a lot of Indonesian students who are also going there to study.'

'Oh, I would want to go to Malang first to talk it over with my father and mother,' he said.

'Forget it, there's no time. Make up your mind quickly. You must have the courage to make a decision.'

'But Mai . . . ?' he said.

'Talk it over with her. She can follow you later. The important thing is for you to go there now.'

That night he could not sleep and tossed about in bed discussing it with Mai. When it was past midnight he finally decided not to go because he felt it was irresponsible to leave Mai in Yogyakarta. Then she urged him strongly to change his mind.

'There's no need to worry about me,' she said to him. 'I'll stay at Father's house again. We have a lot of friends in important republican circles, you don't have to worry.'

So, in the end, he decided to go. He arrived safely in Jakarta and was successful too in being accepted to study in Holland. His Hooger Burger School Diploma facilitated his acceptance because his marks were very high.

After a year in Holland he brought Mai over and later returned to Indonesia as a doctor and settled in Jakarta. While he was in Holland he felt changes going on inside him. It was as if his eyes, his mind and heart were opened to the problems of his people and homeland. In Holland he gained a new understanding of the meaning of a colonized people and colonial powers. He avidly followed the newspapers and read history books and became aware of the crime perpetrated by imperialism and capitalism against the peoples of countries occupied by foreign nations for hundreds of years in various parts of the world. Slowly there emerged an awareness and pride in his nationality. He was an Indonesian. In him flowed the blood of his mother and his mother's mother and so on for several generations past. He became involved actively with Dutch and Indonesian groups in Holland who supported the Indonesian independence struggle. He wrote to his parents telling them of these new ideas and feelings he had. And finally he decided to change his name to an Indonesian name and he told his parents this and asked their permission to do so.

His father wrote back that he would not forbid him to do this. 'Whatever you do,' wrote his father, 'do it with your whole heart.'

He felt his father did not really agree to him changing his name and, full of anxiety for weeks after, he pondered on what he should do. Until finally he felt very confused, and seeing no way out, he talked about his confusion with his friend Syamsuddin, a student in his class.

'Yes, but what do you want to change your name to an Indonesian one for, Tio?' his friend asked. 'Isn't Indonesian society a composite society? The differences between a Javanese and a Papuan are perhaps greater than those between a Javanese and a Chinese, but the important thing is what's inside him, isn't it? If you feel Indonesian, isn't that what's important? Not all Indonesian names are indigenous either, there are Arab, Hindu, Portuguese, Dutch and German names. Imagine it, there are many Christian Bataks with names like Hindenburg, Bremen, Washington, Karel, Westminister....'

They both laughed. And he felt impressed when Syamsuddin said, 'Indonesian people must be proud that we can form a human society living in harmony and peace, composed of different ethnic groups, each with its own unique culture and tradition, thus forming a beautiful carpet of human life, full of all kinds of colours, giving pleasure to all. We don't want to destroy all the regional cultures and make everything the one dead grey colour, do we?'

This convinced him, and he now saw himself as an Indonesian nationalist with all loyalty to his homeland and people, but also proud of the Indonesian and Chinese blood in him. Although he was offered a job in a hospital in Rotterdam, he decided to go home to Indonesia because he was convinced that his life's work and responsibility lay with his own people.

He immediately became well known and popular in the élite circles in Jakarta and also with the common folk. He was well known as a successful doctor. But in less affluent circles he was also well renowned as a doctor who was not at all greedy. On the contrary he was prepared not to ask for anything, if his patients admitted that they could not afford to pay. Often, too, if he had medicine on him, he would give it to his patients free of charge.

His patients came from all groups, those who supported and those who opposed Soekarno. He listened to all their stories about political struggles and upheavals. And he often felt sad at how, during those years that preceded the outbreak of the Gestapu Indonesian Communist Party Incident which brought about the downfall of the Soekarno regime, the struggle for the freedom of the Indonesian people had been diverted by the leaders of the struggle into being a fight to retain individual and faction dominance.

He also became a member of Soekarno's medical team. Almost all of the ministers, many generals and also various figures in the opposition and in parties supporting Soekarno came to him for treatment. He heard their stories and always tried, if the opportunity arose, to gently urge those important men and leaders at that time to put the interests of the common people before those of individuals and groups. Their reactions varied. There were some who said, 'You are right, but the conflict now can no longer be resolved. Every faction wants to win for itself. Soekarno has become president for life. Ousting him from power can only be done by force. The Communist Party also wants a communist dictator. The Muslims and the nationalists are in disarray and the armed forces have been infiltrated by communists.'

Then the Gestapu Indonesian Communist Party incident erupted and was immediately followed by the struggle to topple Soekarno from power. Tio's children, who when they were young all went to Elementary School, then Junior and Senior High School, all joined KAPPI.[1] They let down car tyres, joined in processions and lined up shouting slogans against the old order. One of his children who was at junior high even took part in the attack on the Department of Foreign Affairs under Dr Subandrio, who with hatred was nicknamed 'Durno' because he was wily like the *wayang* character of the same name. The child fell victim to the tear gas used as a security measure against those who wanted to bring the business of the Department to a halt. Very proudly the child brought home a piece of torn curtain from the Foreign Affairs Ministry as a souvenir of the struggle. One of his daughters in Junior High School was chased with her friends by the Cakrabirawa forces in front of the Merdeka Palace.

The whole family now felt involved in the life of the people and felt themselves part of the Indonesian nation. Tio felt happy and very proud to see his children's spirit. In his heart he was a little jealous, because when he was their age he had no feelings at all of the national pride that his children now felt.

He and his children welcomed the victory of the new

[1] Action Front of High School Students and Youth.

order joyfully like most of the Indonesian people did. But later, riots broke out against the Chinese population of Bandung in 1969, which shocked him greatly. In the following years he saw and heard expressions and attitudes which began to be anti-Chinese and often too he experienced various kinds of discrimination in his career as an employee of the Department of Health. It was done in a subtle way, but still he felt that if he was not of Chinese blood those things would not have happened to him. A very clear instance was his position as a civil servant and teacher at the state university. Just seen from the length of time he had worked there, his position in fact should have been higher than it was now, both in the department and the university. But he was always overlooked in the filling of higher posts and these were given to indigenous Indonesian colleagues.

He and Mai often talked about this and he always said to his wife, 'Oh, leave it, Mai. Let's not think it's too bad. We don't expect to live on my salary as a civil servant or a university lecturer, do we? The proceeds from my practice are more than enough.'

'Yes, but it is discrimination, isn't it?' grumbled Mai.

'The discrimination is not really only one-sided,' he said to his wife, 'but if we want to be honest, haven't we Chinese also practised discrimination against the Indonesians since the early days? Just in the matter of marriage, we would very rarely let our girls marry Indonesian men, but vice versa was all right. Only recently has it become more common for our girls to marry them. In the business world also we are happier dealing among ourselves. To make up for our sins all this time, I am prepared to be discriminated against, provided the same thing doesn't happen to our children.'

This had become his conviction because he looked to the future. He wanted to see his children really become Indonesians, members of Indonesian society, the same as everyone else.

He took another long breath, remembering his wife's

message that two of his young children who were still in primary school wanted to tell him something. He looked at the clock on the wall. It was past 1 a.m. His children of course would be asleep and his wife too. Slowly he went into the house, went to the kitchen, poured some cold milk from the refrigerator into a glass and swallowed it in one gulp. After changing from his white coat to his pyjamas he gently lay down beside his wife and whispered softly, 'Mai, are you asleep?'

His wife did not answer; her breathing was regular, the breathing of a person sleeping soundly. He closed his eyes and a moment later he too fell asleep.

Mai opened her eyes and looked at her husband, full of love. She was not asleep; her thoughts were troubled by what her two little children had told her. But she did not want to tell her husband that night. She wanted him to sleep so he could rest from his long, hard work.

Next morning at the breakfast table, the only time they were together, Fifi and Nina told him how the day before they had been teased and abused by their friends who had shouted at them, 'Chinese with the funny voice, Chinese with the funny voice, corrupt Chinese crooks,' and so on, until they started to cry because they felt angry, and finally they stood up to them and had a fight.

'What does "Chinese with a funny voice" mean, Father?' they asked.

He was very shocked by what they said and without realizing it he squeezed the glass of milk he was holding till it broke and pieces of glass scattered on the table and showered on the floor, and milk wet the table-cloth and spilt on the floor. He felt blood oozing from his hand, he went pale and felt tears welling up in his eyes. His breathing was as though constricted, his lips trembled wanting to say something and suddenly a great feeling of sorrow, very heavy and very cold, crumpled his heart and all of his feelings. When he tried to stand up he felt shaky, his knees and legs were wobbly and weak and he fell back again on to the chair. Mai was startled and stood up and asked, 'What's the matter, Tio, are you sick?' And his children sitting around the table looked at him in surprise, their wide eyes fixed on him.

'Oh, it's nothing. I am probably overtired from work,' he finally said slowly after he managed to control himself. 'You go to school and I will talk to the headmaster later,' he said.

The headmaster, a large number of the teachers and their children were his patients, too. After hearing his story the headmaster was very shocked and apologized to him and promised to draw the other teachers' attention to the matter and to ask them to warn all the children not to repeat that sort of behaviour.

'You know yourself, doctor, at Perwari school those in charge and the teachers, all want to educate the children to be true and good Indonesian men and women. I hope you can understand that possibly the children who teased Fifi and Nina had some outside influence and behaved like that without fully realizing it. We will all speak to them. As far as we are concerned, Fifi and Nina are no different from the other pupils.'

Nevertheless Tio still felt disturbed and he found himself examining more closely and with more awareness developments in society. More frequently he read in the newspapers and heard stories from his patients about how members of the Chinese community were increasingly involved in what was called Big Shot Chinese financier connections, the bribing of important people by Chinese businessmen, huge bank credit being given to Chinese financiers without their fulfilling the proper bank conditions because the head man paid a huge kickback too. Among these was the incident of credit bank manipulation for millions of dollars by A. Tjai alias Endang Wijaya and tens if not hundreds of others. He could understand the rise in temperature of the Indonesians' annoyance and anger with characters like that.

But for his innocent children to be treated in that way? He could accept it for himself. He said to himself, 'Let me alone suffer all kinds of discrimination, control myself, submit to defeat, suppress my feelings, put aside my own worries and fears facing this attitude of racial discrimination. But I am not prepared to let my children live like that all their lives, being defeated continually by discrimination against them, losing their courage to defend their rights, losing their self-respect and their human dignity. Do they have to live as people full of fear and subservience all their lives in their own native land?'

He kept these feelings to himself. He didn't dare to convey this dark picture of the children's future to his wife.

Three months later Fifi and Nina came home from school with torn dresses. They had been in another fight with their friends. The same thing had happened again. He took the news very calmly.

'We can't do anything about it, it's our fate,' he said to his children. 'Starting tomorrow you do not have to go to school any more, Fifi and Nina. I am going to send you to school in Holland straight away. You can live with Uncle Go. You will go to school there.'

At first the children refused to go because they preferred living in Indonesia. 'We like school here,' they said, 'only a few children are cruel to us. The others are all nice. In Holland we have no friends.'

Gently he explained to his two little girls that they would only be by themselves for a little while, and very soon Father, Mother and their brothers and sister would follow. The next day the headmaster came and apologized for what had happened.

Patiently he explained to the headmaster that Fifi and Nina were forbidden to go to school and that he was going to send them away.

'But, sir ...', said the headmaster, shocked.

'Unless', he said, 'you are able to expel two or three of those bad children from school!'

The headmaster was frightened. 'Sir, those are the children of very important men. How can I expel them?'

'I understand,' he said, 'because of that, let my children be the ones to leave.'

He explained to the headmaster all of the feelings and thoughts that had disturbed him for so long. The headmaster bowed his head and in a deep voice said, 'I am ashamed, sir. In my heart I weep, but I have no power....'

'I understand. It's not your fault, it's not the fault of the children who tormented Fifi and Nina either. It's our society that is not yet mature and adult enough to live together that's at fault.'

For their first 17 August celebrations in Holland, they were invited to celebrate the proclamation of Indonesian independence. When he lifted his glass to drink the health of the Republic of Indonesia there floated in front of his eyes the dreams and beautiful promises of Indonesian independence about equality and unity of the people. These were quickly replaced by the scene around the dining-table at his house in Jakarta, and without his realizing it, his hand squeezed the glass as he tried to control his suddenly unsteady feelings and the glass broke and hurt his hand. His blood mingled with fruit juice, wet his hand and fingers.

The Cultural Attaché of the Indonesian Embassy, who was standing beside him, offered him his clean, white handkerchief to bandage his injured hand, saying, 'You are feeling very moved by this, aren't you, sir?'

'Yes,' he said, 'I am very moved,' and he and his wife looked at each other.

CHAPTER TWELVE

The Hunt

FOR more than a week the rice fields had been golden-yellow in the Mandailing Valley. The rice stalks were bowed over, swollen and full, ripe in the warmth of the sun's rays. The owners of the fields were very happy. The harvest this year would be wonderful. No diseases had come to attack the rice plants and there had not been many mice either. And for weeks and weeks since the rice started to turn yellow, they had guarded against attacks by sparrows. But the sparrows that did come trying to find rice were also fewer than usual.

The whole Mandailing Valley, with the Batang Gadis River that flowed through it, and the hills thickly grown with rubber trees and guarded by the soaring Sorik Merapi Volcano, were as if smiling in the sunshine. Man and nature around him were so harmonious and united that children and adults, not to mention young people, felt their blood flowing fast and hot. Everywhere children could be heard playing and shouting, youths singing and young girls could be seen glancing at their boy-friends.

The sound of flutes could be heard everywhere in the fields. This was the time when people made plans—betrothal plans and marriage plans, plans to travel and plans to wed with the proceeds of their rice harvest.

At the house of Sutan Gunung Mulia, in the village of Aek Bontar, negotiations had been completed for the marriage of his son Mahmudin, with Siti Maimunah, the daughter of Mahmudin's uncle. Mahmudin was a Lubis and

Maimunah was a Nasution, and this was indeed as it should be in accordance with Mandailing custom and their families' connections.

After the other members of their family who had taken part in the discussions had gone home, Sutan Gunung Mulia called Mahmudin.

'Din, in two days' time we will harvest the rice. It is important for you to see that pigs don't get into the fields.'

'Yes, Father,' Mahmudin answered.

In his heart he was very excited that the date of his marriage to Maimunah had been decided—two weeks after the harvest was finished. Only when he was married would he really become an adult and a full member of the village community. Although his marriage to Maimunah had been arranged by the parents on both sides, he himself liked Maimunah. They had been friends since they were small. His parents often took him to her house and they had been in the same class right through from primary school to junior high. He was nineteen years old, at the peak of his virility. His body felt warm when he thought about the night of his wedding with Maimunah. He and his friends often talked and told stories about sexual intercourse between men and women, and stories and talk like that always made his blood flow fast and he would feel his body getting warm, as if with a slight fever, but it was all pleasurable and disturbing.

Their fields spread along the edge of the Batang Gadis River as far as the foot of the hills that rolled far to the south of their village. The hills were thick with old rubber tree forests that had gone wild, not cared for or cleaned up for who knows how many years. His father said that perhaps the rubber forests in Mandailing were almost one hundred years old, if not more. As far as his father and his grandmother could remember the forests were there when they were born. Behind the rubber forests were many hills overgrown with long grasses and there the villagers opened up un-irrigated fields and land and planted cassava and sweet potato. Behind the grass hills there were forests where the village people went to chop down trees for posts and timber to build their houses.

Elephants and tigers still roamed there and wild pigs came down to the grass hills to eat the cassava and sweet potato. Often, too, they came down to ravage the fields of ripe rice.

Deer also visited the grass hills. The villagers sometimes purposely burnt off the grass on a few hills in the wet season, and when the new, young, green grass grew, the deer liked to come and eat it. Then the villagers hunted the deer. And if the pigs were too great a nuisance to the dry fields and land, they would also hunt them, taking a few hunting-dogs, old rifles, spears and machetes.

Mahmudin loved joining in the hunt. He trained two hunting-dogs that were clever at smelling out the tracks of deer or pigs, barked loudly and fiercely and were courageous when they confronted wild pigs. When the barking of one of the dogs began echoing from hill to hill at the start of the hunt, and they started to chase the dogs after the deer or pigs, and forced a pig to leap out and leave its hiding place, then the thrill of the hunt really became exciting. He would run tirelessly up and down hills till he reached the spot where the dogs had cornered the pig. Then he and his friends would kill the pig with spears and machetes. They preferred ending each hunt that way to shooting a cornered pig. They only killed the deer with rifles. The pleasures of deer-hunting were different. A deer had to be waited for where it came to feed. Mahmudin had been successful twice at hunting deer.

Waiting, not moving a muscle, refraining from smoking, blending into the surroundings, was a different challenge again from pitting the strength of body and the heat of the chase with the hunting-dogs, up and down hills.

Each time he had been successful he had been greeted by the people of his village as a hero. Cheerfully he shared the venison with his friends in the village. And for days and days the young children talked to him about the hunt and the old people acknowledged him and admired his hunting ability.

There was one more hunt that he wanted to do, but the desire to do so was always accompanied by feelings of anxiety and fear. He used to imagine that one day he would hunt a big savage tiger that terrorized the villagers and mauled cattle or goats and humans. And it was he who would come forward and rid the village of the terror of the savage tiger. To succeed in shooting a tiger was a dream for him, and if he did succeed it would be like forming a crown which marked him as a true hunter.

But, although the villagers said that in various places around Mandailing there were still tigers in the forests, none had come down to the village to attack the livestock for a few years, and Mahmudin during this time never got the chance to prove his courage, superiority and skill as the best hunter in his village.

With those kinds of thoughts in his head he looked for his friends, remembering what his father had said about arranging if necessary to chase away the pigs if they came to raid the rice fields.

The second night after the harvest began, a band of wild pigs did come into the fields. Fortunately, before they had a chance to do much damage to the rice, the youths and old people guarding the fields knew of their coming, and with torches, blows and loud shouts and yells, they succeeded in driving the pigs away.

That night also, Mahmudin discussed going pig-hunting with his friends the next day. Ten of them were going. They would bring two rifles, spears, machetes and their hunting-dogs.

The next day, after the dawn prayer, they gathered at Mahmudin's house. Each of them brought food supplies wrapped in banana leaves, then tied firmly around the waist in a sarong.

'Be careful, son,' said his father to Mahmudin when they were about to leave.

A thin mist still covered the early morning when they

crossed the fields and the Batang Gadis River and reached the dimness of the rubber forests in the hills. Their dogs started pulling at the leashes tied around their necks, as they scented the pig tracks. But they did not want to release the dogs too soon. Mahmudin's friends started to tease him.

'Well,' one of them said, 'when you are married, Din, I wonder if you will be able to get up like this to come hunting with us.'

'Hah,' another one added, 'of course, he'll prefer ... hm, hm!'

They laughed. And his friends' teasing made Mahmudin think of Maimunah. 'I wonder what she's doing now?' he asked himself. And he began to day-dream, imagining life with Maimunah, imagining their wedding night and how if they had a child, only then would he really feel that he was a man. Of course he wanted his first child to be a boy, like his father and uncle had had. And then a girl and then another boy. When he had a son, a father had a child to continue his line. A daughter would leave her home and family and become a member of her husband's family. He would work hard and save his money because he wanted to build their house himself. He would try to buy fields and if he accumulated some capital he also wanted to open a stall or a small shop. He wanted their children to go to school. Yes, he would work as hard as he could while the strength of his youth was still in his body, so that their children could be educated right up to university level. His father had not been able to educate him beyond junior high school because he had too many children. There were nine of them and he was the eldest. His mother had had a baby almost every two years, one after the other without stopping.

Now the government had accelerated the family planning programme, and after he was married and after they had three children, he would join in family planning. He wanted his children to be more advanced than he was, more advanced than the life of their family had been from the past to the present day.

He could imagine his and Maimunah's joy and pride if their children succeeded in graduating from university to become doctors or engineers. Swept away in the current of his day-dreams, he was startled when one of his friends shouted in his ear, 'Hei, stop thinking about Maimunah. Where do we go now?'

He started, thrown from his world of day-dreams, and saw that they had arrived at the edge of the rubber forest and before them were spread the grass-covered hills.

His friends laughed. 'Mahmudin thinks he's the only one who has a fiancée and is going to get married soon,' someone cut in, and this made them laugh again. Mahmudin joined in the laughter. After it died down he said it was time for the dogs to be released.

Now the dogs kept sniffing the ground and pig tracks and barking non-stop. The sound of the barking bounced from hill to hill.

'They are so noisy they'll wake up any pigs that are asleep,' someone grumbled.

'That doesn't matter,' said Mahmudin, 'on the contrary it would be good. Let's race them. Ready?' he asked, then he released his dogs and the others followed suit.

Free from the restraint of their leashes, the dogs barked louder, ran round and round a moment in all directions, excited by the scent of the pig tracks and by their awakening hunting spirit, until one of Mahmudin's dogs barked madly and ran off towards the forest across the grass hills. The others followed him immediately. Of course Mahmudin's dogs always led the pack when they went hunting, because they were very well trained.

Mahmudin and his friends followed their dogs, at first walking faster than usual. Then when their hunting blood also began to warm up and flow faster, they started to run quite quickly, and a quarter of an hour later, when they heard their dogs barking loudly and no longer moving away into the distance, they knew that they had found the pig. They increased their pace till they were racing along. The hunting instinct which lies buried in man's soul, inherited from his ancestors, now captured their bodies and urged their feet to run fast, controlling their breathing and sharpening their senses. Their hunting spirit was tremendously stimulated and they felt another excitement, the thrill that arose in the body of a man who ran to meet danger and knew that it was his own choice and was fully convinced that he would prevail over whatever happened.

It was as though their feet had their own eyes, without being told by their brains to leap over holes that could break their legs if they stumbled in them, and skilfully carried them leaping up and down steep banks.

Mahmudin and two of his friends were the first to reach the spot where the dogs had cornered the pig. Knowing that their masters had arrived, the dogs became more fierce and daring. They saw that the wild pig that was cornered was a big male. Its tusks were big and sharp. Its eyes were red, defying the dogs which kept attacking it and then retreating when it lunged back at them.

'Ah, you are a beauty, aren't you,' Mahmudin said softly, getting his spear ready. He signalled his friends to get ready to face the pig's attack. It often happened that if a pig was stabbed by a spear it would forget about the dogs and charge the human that had wounded it. Only dodging fast could save you from a pig's attack. If you were gored by a sharp tusk, the calf of your leg could be sliced open. It was very dangerous. Mahmudin raised his spear and swung his arm as hard as he could and threw the spear at the pig. The barb penetrated its shoulder and it screamed in pain, squealed and swayed and leapt and charged in the direction where Mahmudin and his friends were standing.

'Look out for the pig!' they yelled to warn their friends who had just arrived. The dogs that had cornered it got out of the way of the charging pig, their line broken. Two dogs that did not move quickly enough were knocked down by the huge weight of the pig's body, so they were flung aside yelping with pain. Then the pig was out of the trap and reached the spot where Mahmudin and his friends were. Skilfully they leapt aside and the pig passed them and immediately saw other humans in its path. It stopped suddenly, confused about whether to turn back and attack the men it had just attacked or charge those who had just arrived and were now in front of it.

Its hesitation destroyed it, because Mahmudin quickly sprang and picked up his spear and shouted out, telling his friends to all spear the pig together. Meanwhile the dogs had found their courage again and started to bark and hem the pig in, and one or two of them took turns to attack, closing in on the pig and retreating quickly if it returned their attack.

Four spears hit the pig's body and it fell to the ground and was immediately savaged by the dogs that bit it in several places all at once. The pig still tried to fight, tried to get up again, but it was getting weaker, bleeding all over its body from the spear wounds and dog bites. Then one of the men stabbed the pig's neck with his sharp machete and blood gushed out and sprayed the ground.

Its legs, tail, body and head quivered, and then it lay sprawled on the ground, covered in its own blood. It had paid the debt for stealing the rice of human beings.

They tied the dogs up again and didn't let them eat the pig's flesh because they wanted to continue the hunt.

By about one thirty in the afternoon they had succeeded in finding two more pigs. The second was able to escape after it was speared in the side and the dogs lost its scent because it ran into the swamp at the edge of a big forest. They succeeded in killing the third, after one of the dogs fell victim to its attack.

They were a long way from the village and had reached the edge of a large forest, engrossed in chasing the pigs. They stopped at the edge of a clear, flowing stream full of stones and pebbles and washed their feet and faces. They laughed and retold the story of their very successful hunting, all laughing at each other's behaviour when they faced the charge of the cornered pig. They were breathing normally again and they ate greedily.

'The fields will be safe till the harvest is over,' said Mahmudin. 'I think we've chased away all the pigs in the hills near our village.'

After they had finished eating and were enjoying a cigarette Mahmudin said, 'It's just ridiculous for us to go home now. Why don't we go looking for deer?'

And he explained to his friends where he expected the deer would come out of the forest in the late afternoon. Their thrill of the hunt which was heightened by their success in hunting the pigs, rose again hearing Mahmudin's proposal and they all agreed to it with great excitement.

'Well, in that case we'll leave now,' he said, 'but we'll leave the dogs here. Tie them up to the bushes!'

They left the dogs and set off, heading for the spot Mahmudin had told them about, a field that had been abandoned by the farmer but was overgrown with all sorts of green, leafy plants that deer liked.

An hour later they reached the spot. The hut that the farmer had built previously had long been in ruins. Mahmudin carried one rifle and his friend Bakar, the other.

'From now on we must be quiet. There must be no sound at all,' Mahmudin warned his friends.

Half an hour, an hour, one and a half hours—no deer appeared. Mahmudin felt rather disappointed. If it got too late they would not get back to the village before dark. Half an hour later when still nothing came down from the forest, and just when he was about to suggest that they go home, suddenly someone whispered, 'Shh, is there something moving there?' and pointed towards the forest.

They strained their eyes and their ears. Yes, they heard the sound of a branch being trodden on by something, but did not see anything. Tension started to creep into their bodies. And in Mahmudin's heart someone whispered,

'What if it's a tiger?' For a moment he was frightened, but he calmed down again looking at his friends. Something made a noise again, coming closer, and then the bushes about fifty metres in front of them could be seen moving and they parted and a young buck stepped out followed by two young does.

They held their breath, enchanted by the deer that were so close to them. The buck, whose antlers had just started to branch, turned his head in all directions, carefully noting the situation around him, sniffing the air, and then, feeling safe, stepped forward to the abandoned field and stopped about thirty metres from the spot where Mahmudin and his friends were hiding. Mahmudin and Bakar, who had the rifles, slowly raised them to their shoulders, each taking aim at a deer, and at a signal from Mahmudin they both fired at the same time. The sound of the two rifle shots rent the silence of the abandoned field, echoing to the forest and back, silencing the noise of monkeys calling in the forest and breaking the tension. The buck which Mahmudin had shot at, fell and lay on the ground. The female that Bakar had shot fled, but had only gone a few dozen metres when it fell to the ground, tried to get up again, fell again, and at that moment, full of burning excitement and eagerness, the ten of them leapt up drawing their machetes and ran to where the two deer lay. Smacking their lips, they shouted a victory cry and pranced around the deer.

After their excitement died down they slit the deer's throats and quickly skinned them.

'This is really a good omen for a prospective bridegroom,' Bakar said. 'Imagine, three pigs and two deer in one day. It's never happened before in the history of our village.'

'Two pigs,' put in one of his friends.

'Oh, the other one was wounded, wasn't it? It ran into the swamp. It would have drowned there,' answered Bakar.

'Yes, three pigs and two deer,' they all shouted.

Skilfully they cut up the venison, wrapped it in banana

leaves that were growing wild in the field and tied it with string made from banana stems.

'Now we'd better hurry home,' Mahmudin ordered.

Quickly they set off for the village. Evening was near, and long shadows of trees covered the ground by the time they reached the edge of the slopes of the rubber forest near their village. In the forest it had started to get dark and they hurried, walking quickly. When they saw the rubber trees thinning out and were close to the edge of the forest with the village fields beginning to spread out before them, suddenly someone shouted, 'The last one in the forest will be caught by a tiger,' and ran fast out of the forest and overtook his friends. Then they all ran, each one looking for his own open path between the thickly growing rubber trees. They reached the edge of the forest almost at the same time, jumping a rather steep bank to reach the fields, when suddenly they heard a man's scream of pain, agonizing, heartbreaking, tearing the air, and it was as though a sharp knife had sliced through them.

They stopped as if pulled up in their tracks by the hand of a powerful giant. They looked at each other, all the excitement that had filled them draining from their bodies and leaving them quite empty.

'Mahmudin, oh god, where is Mahmudin?' they almost screamed.

They looked for him straight away, and then—'Oh God, God protect us, oh God,' was all they could say as they stood at the edge of a pit, with sharpened bamboo spikes stuck in it, that the villagers had dug at the edge of the forest to catch pigs.

Mahmudin lay sprawled in the pit, a spike sticking out of his chest, his eyes wide open looking at them, but not seeing them any more.

'We are God's and to Him we return,' was all they could say, with strained voices, sobbing to themselves.

No one dared to think about the rest of this day when

later the villagers heard what happened. Bakar got down into the pit, picked up the rifle that had fallen from Mahmudin's hand, and the package of meat he had carried and pulled out the other spikes. Two of the others got down and they lifted Mahmudin's body out of the pit. In his heart that was full of sorrow for his friend who should be looking forward to his joyful wedding day, Bakar could not imagine what Maimunah and Mahmudin's parents would feel, and he did not know what he would say to them.

'We surrender to you, oh God,' he said to himself as he and his friends all carried Mahmudin's body into the village and dropped their rifles and packages of venison to the ground.

Some other Oxford Paperbacks for readers interested in Central Asia,
China and South-East Asia, past and present

CAMBODIA

GEORGE COEDÈS
Angkor

MALCOLM MacDONALD
Angkor and the Khmers*

CENTRAL ASIA

ANDRÉ GUIBAUT
Tibetan Venture

PETER FLEMING
Bayonets to Lhasa

LADY MACARTNEY
An English Lady in Chinese
Turkestan

DIANA SHIPTON
The Antique Land

C. P. SKRINE AND
PAMELA NIGHTINGALE
Macartney at Kashgar*

ALBERT VON LE COQ
Buried Treasures of Chinese
Turkestan

AITCHEN K. WU
Turkistan Tumult

CHINA

All About Shanghai: A Standard
Guide

HAROLD ACTON
Peonies and Ponies

VICKI BAUM
Shanghai '37

ERNEST BRAMAH
Kai Lung's Golden Hours*

ERNEST BRAMAH
The Wallet of Kai Lung*

ANN BRIDGE
The Ginger Griffin

CHANG HSIN-HAI
The Fabulous Concubine*

CARL CROW
Handbook for China

PETER FLEMING
The Siege at Peking

MARY HOOKER
Behind the Scenes in Peking

CORRINNE LAMB
The Chinese Festive Board

W. SOMERSET
MAUGHAM
On a Chinese Screen*

G. E. MORRISON
An Australian in China

PETER QUENNELL
Superficial Journey through
Tokyo and Peking

OSBERT SITWELL
Escape with Me! An Oriental
Sketch-book

J. A. TURNER
Kwang Tung or Five Years in
South China

HONG KONG AND
MACAU

AUSTIN COATES
City of Broken Promises

AUSTIN COATES
A Macao Narrative

AUSTIN COATES
Myself a Mandarin

AUSTIN COATES
The Road

The Hong Kong Guide 1893

INDONESIA

S. TAKDIR
ALISJAHBANA
Indonesia: Social and Cultural
Revolution

DAVID ATTENBOROUGH
Zoo Quest for a Dragon*

VICKI BAUM
A Tale from Bali*

'BENGAL CIVILIAN'
Rambles in Java and the Straits
in 1852

MIGUEL COVARRUBIAS
Island of Bali*

BERYL DE ZOETE AND
WALTER SPIES
Dance and Drama in Bali

AUGUSTA DE WIT
Java: Facts and Fancies

JACQUES DUMARÇAY
Borobudur

JACQUES DUMARÇAY
The Temples of Java

ANNA FORBES
Unbeaten Tracks in Islands of the
Far East

GEOFFREY GORER
Bali and Angkor

JENNIFER LINDSAY
Javanese Gamelan

EDWIN M. LOEB
Sumatra: Its History and People

MOCHTAR LUBIS
The Outlaw and Other Stories

MOCHTAR LUBIS
Twilight in Djakarta

MADELON H. LULOFS
Coolie*

MADELON H. LULOFS
Rubber

COLIN McPHEE
A House in Bali*

ERIC MJOBERG
Forest Life and Adventures in the
Malay Archipelago

HICKMAN POWELL
The Last Paradise

E. R. SCIDMORE
Java, The Garden of the East

MICHAEL SMITHIES
Yogyakarta: Cultural Heart of
Indonesia

LADISLAO SZÉKELY
Tropic Fever: The Adventures of
a Planter in Sumatra

EDWARD C. VAN NESS
AND SHITA
PRAWIROHARDJO
Javanese Wayang Kulit

MALAYSIA

ISABELLA L. BIRD
The Golden Chersonese: Travels
in Malaya in 1879

MARGARET BROOKE
THE RANEE OF
SARAWAK
My Life in Sarawak

HENRI FAUCONNIER
The Soul of Malaya

W. R. GEDDES
Nine Dayak Nights

A. G. GLENISTER
The Birds of the Malay Peninsula,
Singapore and Penang

C. W. HARRISON
Illustrated Guide to the Federated
Malay States (1923)

BARBARA HARRISSON
Orang-Utan

TOM HARRISSON
World Within: A Borneo Story

CHARLES HOSE
The Field-Book of a Jungle-Wallah

EMILY INNES
The Chersonese with the
Gilding Off

W. SOMERSET
MAUGHAM
Ah King and Other Stories*

W. SOMERSET
MAUGHAM
The Casuarina Tree*

MARY McMINNIES
The Flying Fox*

ROBERT PAYNE
The White Rajahs of Sarawak

OWEN RUTTER
The Pirate Wind

ROBERT W. SHELFORD
A Naturalist in Borneo

CARVETH WELLS
Six Years in the Malay Jungle

SINGAPORE

RUSSELL GRENFELL
Main Fleet to Singapore

R. W. E. HARPER AND
HARRY MILLER
Singapore Mutiny

JANET LIM
Sold for Silver

G. M. REITH
Handbook to Singapore (1907)

C. E. WURTZBURG
Raffles of the Eastern Isles

THAILAND

CARL BOCK
Temples and Elephants

REGINALD CAMPBELL
Teak-Wallah

MALCOLM SMITH
A Physician at the Court of Siam

ERNEST YOUNG
The Kingdom of the Yellow Robe

Titles marked with an asterisk have restricted rights.